GHOSTLIGHT

ALSO BY SONIA GENSLER

The Dark Between

The Revenant

GHOSTLIGHT

SONIA GENSLER

ALFRED A. KNOPF
NEW YORK

THIS IS A BORZOI BOOK PUBLISHED BY ALFRED A. KNOPF

Visit us on the Web! randomhousekids.com

Educators and librarians, for a variety of teaching tools, visit us at RHTeachersLibrarians.com

Library of Congress Cataloging-in-Publication Data
Gensler, Sonia.
Ghostlight / Sonia Gensler. — First edition.
p. cm.
Summary: A summer film project turns spooky when the setting turns out to actually be haunted.
ISBN 978-0-553-52214-3 (trade) — ISBN 978-0-553-52215-0 (lib. bdg.) — ISBN 978-0-553-52216-7 (ebook)
[1. Ghosts—Fiction. 2. Haunted houses—Fiction. 3. Motion pictures—Production and direction—Fiction.] I. Title.
PZ7.G29177Gh 2015
[Fic]—dc23
2014039521

The text of this book is set in 11.5-point Apolline.

Printed in the United States of America
August 2015
10 9 8 7 6 5 4 3 2 1

First Edition

For my dear grandmothers, Ruby and Margaret Ellen, who indulged me with stories of the "olden days" and never, ever gave wallopings

CHAPTER 1

We'd only been at Grandma's for *five minutes* before Blake ruined everything.

"I start high school this fall, Avery."

"Duh, I know. So what?"

"So, it means I'm done playing magical kingdoms." He patted his overstuffed backpack. "Besides, I have a mile-long list of summer reading."

At first I just stood there with my mouth hanging open. Then anger boiled in my belly, bubbling higher and higher until it burst from my mouth as the filthiest string of words I'd ever spoken. There was no way to claim I didn't hear Grandma calling after me as I ran off, so I let the screen door slam behind me. Figured I might as well go out in a blaze of glory.

I marched along the gravel driveway toward the back buildings, biting my lip to keep from crying. People always did that in books, but it turns out that biting your lip while stomping is a bad idea. After a quick check for blood, I stepped up my pace. *Stomp, stomp* past the storage shed and the old barn, past the cattail pond and the copper beech tree. I was determined to keep stomping until I hit a fence or a gully. And if it was a gully, I might just jump in. Blake would be sorry then.

I got so caught up imagining my brother kneeling at my grave—blubbering and begging for forgiveness—that I almost stomped straight into the strange boy walking ahead of me. I barely had time to dodge behind a tree before he paused and glanced behind him.

He was shorter than Blake, and skinnier, but seemed around the same age. His button-down shirt was bright white, and his khakis were creased in all the right places. They were city clothes, too nice for summer on a Tennessee farm. He carried a fancy camera with a huge lens, and as he walked, he raised it every few seconds to take a photo. That's probably why he hadn't noticed me.

So I followed him.

I figured I'd have to be stealthy and keep a certain distance. Maybe slip behind a few more trees. But he was oblivious to me because he was taking pictures of *everything*. Trees, bushes, fence posts. He even took a shot of a pile of manure.

I was concentrating pretty hard on him not paying attention to where he was going, which meant I wasn't paying much attention either. When I finally looked past him to what was ahead, I realized his path would take us toward the river.

And that meant we would run right into Hilliard House.

Sure enough, we came through a thicket of trees, and there it stood at the top of the hill, facing away from us toward the river. The redbrick house glowed like an autumn leaf against the blue sky, but its border of bushy, sunburned weeds reminded me of a dirty beard. The churning in my gut started up again.

Ahead of me the strange kid lowered his camera. Then he made a beeline for the house.

"Hey!" I shouted.

He froze in place. After a moment he turned slowly. "Hey *what?*"

"You gotta stay away from there."

"Why?"

His raised eyebrow told me he wasn't used to hearing *no,* so I used my bossy grown-up voice. "This is my grandma's land, and you don't have permission to be on it."

He pointed at Hilliard House. "Is that where she lives?"

"Of course not! Nobody's lived there for ages."

He stared at it for a moment before turning back to me. "So what's the problem? It's a *house.* I'm not going to break it."

"It's just . . . forbidden."

"Seriously?" He grinned. "Is there a curse on it or something?"

I shot him a withering look, Grandma-style. "Forget the house. What's up with that camera? Are you a photographer?"

"No . . . I make movies." He stood a little straighter. "I'm a filmmaker."

That I didn't expect. It was the sort of thing you'd hear from an old dude with a goatee and black-rimmed glasses. In the city. Not from some kid trespassing on a farm.

"What kind of films do you make?" I asked.

"The kind few people understand or appreciate." He glanced back at the house. "So, is it from Civil War times?"

I sighed. "I'm not sure."

"Have you ever been inside?"

"I told you, it's off-limits."

He stared at the house like he was trying to memorize every angle of it. "Didn't you ever look at a place, *really* look at it, and know it had stories to tell?" His eyes met mine. "So many stories that your head felt like it would explode?"

I couldn't look away. "Actually, *yeah*."

"I wonder if the door is locked."

Before I could answer, he took off toward the house, and all I could do was follow as he made his way around to the front porch. His city shoes clacked on the brick-lined path, and my mouth got that tingly, slobbery feeling, like I was about to throw up. I wanted to shush that clacking, as if someone else might hear it. When he leapt up the porch steps to try the front door, I held my breath. But after a few twists of the knob, he shrugged and let go, turning back toward me and stepping more carefully on the way down. He took a few more shots of the house and then walked back to where I stood.

"It's locked up pretty tight." His camera beeped as he checked the photos. When he raised his eyes to me, his expression softened. "Are you sick or something? You look kind of pale."

I swallowed and shook my head. "I'm fine. Why are you here, anyway? I know you're not a local."

"I'm from Nashville, but my dad's renting a little white house down the road."

I nodded. "That's Hollyhock Cottage—it belongs to my grandma. You here for the summer?"

"Dad is. As for me . . . I'm not sure."

"And you're thinking of making a *movie* out here?"

"Maybe." He pushed more buttons on his camera. "I'd love to take more footage of this place, from all different angles."

"I have to get back now. Grandma's expecting me."

What Grandma was expecting was to chew me out for swearing at Blake and slamming the door, but I wasn't about to mention that. I just wanted to get some distance between me and Hilliard House.

"Okay. See you later." He pointed his camera toward the house and fiddled with the lens.

"Um, that means you have to go, too," I said, "seeing as you're trespassing and all."

He didn't have a quick answer for that. When he lowered the camera, his green eyes gleamed with . . . well, I wasn't quite sure what, but it was something bright and alive.

I thought of Blake and how his face had lost all of its liveliness over the past few months. There was a time when it was no big deal for him to smile or laugh or just seem *excited* in some way. Now he always looked bored. It didn't help that his hair drooped into his eyes most of the time.

This kid, on the other hand, seemed like he could barely contain himself.

"It's such a cool old building," he said.

"There's plenty more on this farm I could show you. Places much better than an old, falling-down house."

"Yeah?"

"I could come down to the cottage tomorrow after lunch and give you the tour, if you want."

He frowned. "It'd be easier if I met you. You live in that house at the top of the hill, right? I could meet you at one o'clock and we could scout locations together."

I wasn't sure what that meant, but it sounded a heck of a lot better than sitting alone in my attic bedroom plotting Blake's unsolvable murder.

"Sounds cool. I'm Avery, by the way. Avery Hilliard. My family's owned this land for about a million years." I grinned. "Or thereabouts."

"I'm Julian." His gaze shifted to the left. "Just Julian."

When I got back to the house, Grandma was settled in the saggy brown couch, a smile curving her mouth. I wasn't fooled.

"Sorry about slamming the door and all," I mumbled.

"Sit down, Avery May." She patted the space next to her.

Weasley was stretched out on the rug, so I scooped him up before I sat down. Not that I needed protection from Grandma or anything. I just knew she was irked, and it felt good to have something warm and furry to hold on to.

"I wish you'd try to put yourself in Blake's shoes," Grandma said. "He's nearly fifteen and has different interests, but he doesn't have the words for expressing that in a kindly way. He will learn, however, and it's your mother's job—and mine—to keep at him. Not yours."

"But we had plans for Kingdom this summer. We were going to get Princess Etheline married to the Lord of the North Countries, remember? Blake was supposed to write the treaty, and I was writing the vows."

"Honestly, child, I'm surprised he stuck with Kingdom for as long as he did. You might be grateful for that."

My eyeballs were prickling, so I concentrated hard on smoothing Weasley's whiskers. "It's not fair," I muttered. "There's not much to do around here without Kingdom, and I can't keep it going without him."

"Your mama didn't have a brother when she was growing up," Grandma said. "And you know what she did? She used her imagination and found her own projects. Ponder that. You can't go looking to Blake for your happiness."

"Only because he's a jerk."

Her mouth tightened. "People who can entertain themselves draw others to them."

I lowered my head and tried to look repentant, but really I was thinking of Julian and his quest for the perfect film location.

"I met a boy today, Grandma. He said he's staying at Hollyhock Cottage."

She nodded. "A gentleman took the house a couple of days ago. I believe he brought his son with him." She gave me a sidelong look. "You ought to come with me when I check on them tomorrow morning. I need to meet this boy if you're going to be spending time with him."

"It's not as if I *like* him or anything. He's a little weird."

"I'll reach my own conclusions about that. In the meantime, you're washing the dishes for the rest of this week." She smiled. "And I've put my cheesy lasagna in the oven, so you'd best gird your loins for battle."

"Grandma," I whispered. "I wish you wouldn't say *loins*."

CHAPTER 2

I did an excellent job of ignoring Blake at dinner that night, but afterward I must have been banging pans in the dishwater because Grandma gave me the stink eye as she walked past the kitchen.

The next morning, Blake actually took it upon himself to *talk* to me while we worked in the garden. I'd been focusing every ounce of my attention on the ripeness of the peas, so it threw me a little when I heard him scramble to his feet and speak from the next row.

"Hey, check out this caterpillar. It's got spikes on it, like it's wearing armor."

I kept my eyes firmly locked on the peas and didn't say a word.

"Earth to Avery—I'm trying to show you something."

I dropped a handful of pea pods into my bucket.

"Are you still mad about Kingdom?"

Blake doesn't exist. Blake is nothing.

After a moment he sighed. "Real mature, sis."

"Not like you," I snapped. "You're *way* out of my league."

His gloating laugh made me wish I'd kept my mouth shut. But, hey, at least I had a life. While Blake was stuck in the house with nothing but his summer-reading list and a pile of stupid football magazines, I'd be *scouting locations* with Julian. But first I had to make an official welcome visit to Hollyhock Cottage with Grandma.

I always looked forward to visiting the cottage, even if it was just for cleaning and collecting bed linens between tenants. It was sweet and friendly, with its white wood siding and blue trim, not to mention the clusters of tall pink and white flowers bordering the wide porch. It didn't sit as high on the hill as Grandma's house, but it had two full stories and a detached two-car garage.

Grandma gave me the once-over as she rang the doorbell. "Stand up straight, Avery May." Once I'd pulled my shoulders back to her satisfaction, she smoothed her face into a pleasant smile.

The door opened promptly. A man with white teeth and movie-star hair smiled back at us. "Well, hello, Mrs. Hilliard. It sure is a pleasure to see you."

"The pleasure is all mine," Grandma said. "Mr. Wayne, allow me to introduce my granddaughter, Avery May."

I extended my hand. "Pleased to meet you, sir." His palm was dry and smooth, but his fingers had calluses.

"Likewise," he said. "You can call me Curtis if you like."

I could practically hear Grandma's eyebrows leap upward.

"I'm certain Avery May would feel it proper to address you as Mr. Wayne," she said.

"As you wish." He snuck a wink at me. "Come on in. It's much cooler in the house."

Everything about Curtis Wayne seemed expensive. His jeans were soft and distressed in that artistic way that "reeked of boutique," as Mom would say. His hair had blond streaks, and he'd used product to make it stick out in all the right places. He was tanned, but his color was so even I figured it didn't actually come from the sun. If he'd been rude to me, or scary, I'd have said he looked like a Ken doll who'd inherited Barbie's millions. But his wink had seemed real—like he and I were on the cool team and Grandma, with her prissy manners and church clothes, just wasn't.

He led us into the living room and toward the brown sectional couch and braided rug. Mr. Wayne had added his own touch by placing a wooden chair and music stand in front of the window. A guitar stood next to the chair. I didn't know much about guitars, but this one seemed well loved. I mean, it didn't look *new*—there were places where the finish had worn away—but it didn't have any nicks or dust on it. All I could think was that it looked *healthy,* like it got plenty of exercise and was proud of itself.

"Julian's upstairs," he said. "I know he's eager to meet you, Mrs. Hilliard." He gestured toward the couch. "Have a seat while I go unearth him."

Once Mr. Wayne had left the room, Grandma eased herself onto the edge of the sectional. "How refreshing that he did not bellow up the stairs at the boy. I appreciate his manners."

I took the spot next to her and looked around the room for more clues about Julian. The house smelled *male,* but not in a disgusting way, like Blake's sneakers. I caught the spicy whiff of men's deodorant and hair products, the scent of leather, coffee, and other mysterious male things. Nothing flowery or powdery. Where was *Mrs.* Wayne?

Julian came down the stairs first, wearing baggy shorts like a regular kid. His T-shirt had a cartoon of a bearded man with a really high forehead and angry black eyebrows. I'd have asked him about that, but he only looked my way for a second. Even then I saw the jitters in his eyes.

What did *he* have to fear? His dad wasn't embarrassing, and my grandmother couldn't be that scary. When Mr. Wayne nudged his shoulder, Julian stepped forward and offered his hand to Grandma.

"Pleased to meet you, Mrs. Hilliard. I'm Julian. I should have introduced myself yesterday, but I lost my way on your property. Avery was nice enough to show me around."

Grandma smiled and gave his hand a dainty shake. "I hope you'll be staying on the hill the whole summer, Julian. Every year Avery May and her brother come all the way from Dallas to visit, but until now they've never had anyone their age nearby. Usually we get retired couples or writers on retreat at the cottage." She turned to Mr. Wayne. "You're our very first musician. I hope you'll consider joining us at Sycamore Road Church of Christ this summer. The congregation would be honored to hear you sing."

"That's awfully kind of you, Mrs. Hilliard," he said. "I'm quite fond of hymns. I started out singing in church, you know."

Grandma leaned forward. "Did you really?"

"Best training I could have had. I even toured with a Christian group when Julian was little, and he used to sing with us from time to time. Good work for the soul, but not so great for the bank account."

"Oh, I see." Grandma took a breath and smiled again.

"Do you have grand plans for the summer? Any questions I can answer?"

Mr. Wayne took a seat on the sectional, his body lean and supple like a cat's—if a cat could sit upright and rest its paw on an armrest. Julian joined him, but he perched stiffly on the edge, similar to Grandma and me. I tried to send him a smile that said "This stinks, right?" but his jittery look didn't soften.

"My plan for the summer," said Mr. Wayne, "is to get some songs written. I need a place without distractions. No cable TV, no Wi-Fi. Your neck of the woods is perfect, and Julian needs a break from the city, too." He didn't even glance at Julian when he said that last bit, which I found interesting.

Grandma nodded. "And will your wife be joining you?"

Most of the time Grandma's personal questions made me squirm, but this once I appreciated her nosiness. I wanted to know, too.

Mr. Wayne didn't bat an eye. "My wife is a record producer, and she's booked up with studio sessions this summer. Our daughter should be coming soon, though. Lily's swim camp just ended, and she needs a space where she can run wild without distracting her mother. She's only eight."

For a second I'd perked up at the idea of another girl coming to our hill, but eight was practically a baby. And with Julian acting so strange, I was starting to wonder if I'd be on my own for the summer after all.

Julian spoke then, and his voice was so unexpected and loud that I nearly jumped.

"Dad, can I show Avery something in my room? It won't take long."

Mr. Wayne glanced from him to me and smiled. "Assuming it's okay with Mrs. Hilliard. Just keep the door open."

"*Dad.*"

"Be back in ten minutes, Avery May," Grandma said. "I can answer all Mr. Wayne's questions about the house during that time, and then we'll have to move along."

Julian practically bolted for the stairs, and after a quick nod at Grandma, I followed him. Obviously I'd been in Hollyhock Cottage many times before, but his room still managed to surprise me. The single bed was pushed against the wall on one side of the room—no big deal there. But the opposite wall looked like a display in an electronics store. A laptop sat on a wide desk with a massive external hard drive plugged into its left side. A monitor the size of a wide-screen TV sat at the center of the desk. The leftover desk space was filled with Julian's camera and all sorts of other expensive-looking gadgets peeking out of padded cases. Wires and outlet strips snaked across the floor. Everything seemed to hum and flash and give off heat. A plump leather office chair faced us, as if waiting to fold Julian in its arms.

He obliged by slumping into it. "Okay, first of all, do you need to scream or something? If so, just get it over with."

"What do you mean? I've been in a boy's room before."

"I mean my dad."

"What about him? He seems okay."

He studied me for a long moment, like some interrogator from a spy movie. "Are you messing with me?"

"Messing how?"

"Oh, come on. Curtis Wayne? *Country music star* Curtis Wayne?"

"Country music? I never listen to that stuff."

His body actually crumpled a little, and I wondered if I was going to have to call for help or do CPR. It turned out to be a good kind of crumpling, though. It finally forced the jittery look off his face.

"You're being serious?"

"I guess his name sounds familiar," I said. "But I don't pay much attention to who's who in country music."

"Wow. I mean . . . that's great. I get so sick of people talking about him at school." He shrugged. "I know it's stupid, but I was hoping you'd never have to meet him. I didn't want to be 'Curtis Wayne's son' to you."

"Is that why you asked me up here? To rant about your dad?"

I sounded crabby, I know. It's just . . . I'd be sitting pretty if the only confession I had to make about my dad was that he was *famous*.

"Actually, I wanted to show you something. Pull that chair over here by the computer." He jiggled his mouse and opened a gallery of thumbnails, clicking on the first one. "Check out this photo."

"That's Hilliard House," I said, leaning closer. "But . . . you didn't take this yesterday. It's dark outside."

"I snuck out there last night. Don't tell my dad."

At any other time I would have smiled at that—a shared secret was the cornerstone of friendship—but looking at that photo made me think of Grandma's rules about Hilliard House. More important, Grandma's biblical levels of *wrath* when she learned I'd broken those rules. Still, I couldn't help staring at the shot. Julian must have been standing on the road in front, so the house seemed tall and spooky. Behind it the sky was a swirl of black and gold.

"I didn't want to use the flash, so I took my tripod. It looks cool, doesn't it?"

"I guess."

He clicked through a few more photos—all pretty much the same as the first, but from different angles. "There's one in particular I want to show you," he said. "It's the best of all, but it's a little creepy."

I was already creeped out by the thought of Grandma learning I'd followed Julian to Hilliard House. I didn't think another photo would make a difference.

It did.

"You see it?" he asked.

Of course I did, and it made my throat close up. A light glowed faintly in the first-floor window, the one to the far left of the front door.

I turned to him, my face a little hot. "What did you do?"

"I didn't do anything."

"You must have got inside somehow."

He leaned back in his chair, the ghost of a smile playing at his lips. "It freaks you out a little, doesn't it?"

I swallowed a few times and looked at the photo again. "What is it? Some flash effect?"

"I wasn't using a flash, remember? And it's not a reflection. It's like someone lit a lamp in that room." He clicked his mouse again. "But the light is gone in the rest of the shots."

"Julian, why are you showing me all this?"

He clicked back to the photo with the light in the window. "I stayed up half the night thinking about this house. It might just work. In fact, I think it could be *perfect*."

My belly did a backflip. "Perfect for what?"

"For our film, of course."

CHAPTER 3

Ordinarily, just the *mention* of Hilliard House made my stomach twitch and roil. Seeing it yesterday, and now, looking at Julian's photos, was really starting to mess with my head.

The strange thing was that I couldn't remember exactly why it affected me that way. I guess Grandma's anger was a part of it. She'd forbidden us to go there, and the one time I got caught breaking her rule I'd paid dearly for it. But there was something else on top of that—a memory that floated just out of reach, like dandelion fluff on the breeze. Or maybe it was more like a shadow that followed me but never could be faced straight on.

"Hold on a second," I said. "I already told you there are lots better places on the farm for filming than that."

"Like what? I can't imagine any place cooler than that old house."

I thought for a minute how to explain all the locations of Kingdom—magical and completely scare-free places—but then shook my head. "It's better if I show you. Telling you just isn't the same."

He studied his computer screen. "But I was really hoping . . ."

"What?"

He scrolled through the photos one more time before taking a breath and facing me again. "No, you're right. I should see all the options before we get started." He grabbed his camera and pulled the strap over his head. "You do want to make a movie with me, right? Dad says I get a little carried away sometimes."

"Yeah, it'd be super cool to make a movie. It's just . . . I've never filmed anything before. I'm more of a writer."

"It's the same thing, pretty much. It's all storytelling." He checked the little screen on his camera before turning back to me. "You have favorite writers, don't you?"

I nodded.

"Well, I have favorite directors. That's why I'm wearing this shirt."

I pointed to it. "*That's* a movie director? It looks more like a serial killer. My brother would probably wear a shirt like that."

"It's Stanley Kubrick. You know, 2001: *A Space Odyssey*? *A Clockwork Orange*?"

I had no clue what he was talking about, so I just shrugged.

His eyes narrowed. "They're classic films. How old are you, anyway?"

"Thirteen." In, like, ten and a half months. Close enough.

"Well, I only watched *A Clockwork Orange* after my cousin downloaded it. My dad would freak because it's super creepy." He stood up. "So, you want to show me these fabulous story locations now?"

Grandma reminded me I was due back at the house for lunch, so after politely saying good-bye and thanks to Mr. Wayne, I took Julian straight to the old cow barn.

The cows, who'd never shown much in the way of good taste, were fond of the new prefab barn near the house. Blake and I preferred the old half-ruined barn in the lower pasture, because on the inside it looked kind of medieval. Grandma said it looked that way because it was built like old English tithe barns, but on a smaller scale.

Julian stared up at it. "I don't mean to be rude, but, seriously?"

"I know it seems like a cruddy old barn, but look inside. Does it remind you of anything?"

He walked through the wide doorway and looked around. Then he looked again through his camera lens.

"It, um, reminds me of . . . a *barn?*"

"But look at those beams," I said. "They're like arches. The first time we explored this place, Blake said it looked like a medieval hall. You know, for feasting and stuff? Like the Knights of the Round Table?"

"Interesting." Julian took another look through his camera and clicked a few times. "It's not my image of Camelot, but I could see Lancelot and Guinevere secretly meeting in a place like this."

I smiled.

"But we can't film here," he said. "Too many obstacles. For one thing, the lighting is awful."

I peered at the images over his shoulder. They did seem pretty dark. "What if I brought in some candles?"

Only problem was how to sneak them out of the house. Grandma would never give the okay for fire in the old barn.

Julian shook his head. "What else have you got?"

Our next stop was the cattail pond on the other side of the hill, the one Blake and I had named the Mystical Pool. Huge oak trees shaded it, and at one end was a thick cluster of cattails—tall, bushy, and regal. Blake and I had swum in this pond a few times, totally against Grandma's rules. The muddy bottom had slurped and sucked at my feet, and one time Blake came out of the water with two leeches on his right leg. We never swam there again after that, but in our stories the pond became a magical body of water from which King Stanmore's first wife arose and offered him the gift of a charmed sword . . . and her love.

As we drew near, about a hundred frogs squeaked and leapt into the water. Two turtles sunning on a dead branch slid under the surface with a plop. Their ripples widened until the water was smooth again.

I gestured at the pond with a flourish. "Pretty cool, huh?"

Julian studied it from one end to the other, and then checked it through his camera, same as with the barn. "It has an interesting quality to it," he finally said. "A little eerie."

I looked back at the pond. *Eerie?* Well, there were the leeches, but I hadn't planned on telling him about that.

"If we wait here long enough," I whispered, "the turtles and frogs will come back out."

Julian frowned. "Maybe another time. What else have you got?"

Grandma would have called him a "tough customer," but I'd been saving the best for last.

The copper beech tree was very old, very tall, and its branches drooped all the way to the ground. If you parted them, you walked into a space almost like a tepee, only not so dark and close—light and air could still filter in. The floor was cool dirt, making it a great place for escaping the heat and stickiness of a July day, and the leafy roof offered protection from the rain. In Kingdom, this was where the friendly badger family lived, and where Princess Etheline escaped when life at court grew boring, or worse, *dangerous.*

I parted the branches and waved Julian in. After a worried glance at me, he hugged his camera to his body and stepped inside.

"You can still stand under the branches when you're close to the trunk," I said, "but I like to sit. It cools me down. And then, when the sun shines directly through those dark red leaves, it's like the sky is on fire."

He lowered his backpack to the ground and sat next to me, his forehead wrinkling a little as he checked the scene through his camera. "Again, the lighting is a problem."

"But I bet you never thought of filming under a tree before. It's . . ." I scrambled for the right phrase, "out of the ordinary."

He nodded. "Okay. But what sort of story would take place here? I'm not filming a Narnia movie."

He might as well have kicked me. "What could be cooler than a Narnia movie?"

His eyes softened in a familiar way, as if he found me quaint. "It's an interesting place, Avery, but not practical. Anything else?"

"Well . . . there's bits of forest here and there that are kind of wild and old-timey."

"Like what we walked through to get to Hilliard House?"

I nodded slowly.

"There's the river, too," he said. "We could make good use of that."

"So what are you saying?" My stomach already seemed to know the answer, because it was churning again.

"I appreciate the tour, Avery, but Hilliard House is still the best option. All you have to do is look at that house and the stories start telling themselves."

"But I can't go there."

Julian studied me. "What's your deal with that place?"

"I hate talking about it. The last time I was at the house . . ."

How best to explain it? The only people who knew about that day were Grandma, Blake, and me. We never even told Mom the whole story.

"The last time you were at the house *what*?"

I swallowed. "I snuck inside without permission, and Grandma found out."

"So? Did she make you stand in a corner or something?"

"No, Julian, she took a belt to my backside. In my whole life, that's the only time she ever laid a hand on me. It was *serious*."

He was quiet for a moment. "But why?"

"She says Hilliard House is a dangerous place."

There was more to it than that, but it was too weird to say

out loud. It wasn't just that I'd snuck into the house—I'd actually fallen asleep for hours. Grandma called the sheriff and begged him to put together a search party. After they found me, she said I'd wasted the time of a lot of hardworking men. I had to stay in her sight for the rest of the summer. That was when Kingdom started. I couldn't really go anywhere, so we had to pretend.

But if I told Julian that, he'd ask why I went to the house in the first place. And I wouldn't be able to answer. The answer to that question was the shadow I could never see straight on.

"Avery?"

I looked up at Julian. "Sorry, I was just thinking."

"How long ago did you sneak into the house?"

"Oh, it was years ago."

He looked thoughtful. "You're not a little kid anymore, you know."

"She would still kill me."

"Then we'll get in and out without her ever knowing."

My heart lurched. "Were you even listening to me?"

"It's no big deal, I promise. We just have some planning to do first. Can you meet me here tomorrow?"

"Tomorrow's Sunday. There's church and Grandma's Bible lesson and all that. We're not supposed to go visiting on Sundays."

"Okay. Monday, then. In the meantime, you could do some work for the film." He leaned forward. "Since you're spending all day with your grandma tomorrow, ask her when Hilliard House was built and why nobody lives there anymore. Try to find out everything she knows about the place."

I shook my head. "She'll get suspicious for sure."

"Not if you ask the questions in the right way."

"I don't want to get in trouble again."

Julian was quiet for a moment.

"Storytellers are artists," he finally said, "and every artist has to take risks." He held my gaze. "Trust me, it's a super-cool film location. And you're a local expert. I need you on this, Avery."

CHAPTER 4

Grandma's church had the skimpiest congregation I'd ever seen. *Twelve* people, and none of them younger than her. It was a very conservative church, too, which meant the women only opened their mouths during the hymns. Grandma sure liked to belt it out when it came time to sing, but she had a little trouble staying in tempo. I asked her once why the church didn't have a piano, and Grandma said, "We only offer the fruit of our lips in praise, Avery May. There's no need to add instruments to what Christ's spirit made perfect."

I just happened to think a piano would keep everyone on track, not to mention liven things up a bit. She didn't care to hear that, though.

After the service, Grandma drove us home for kitchen-table Sunday school, seeing as Sycamore Road Church of Christ didn't exactly cater to kids. When the lesson came to an end, Grandma said a long and meaningful prayer that stirred up a decent amount of spiritual feeling in me. Then, *finally,* it was time for lunch.

Which was good, because I was starving. But it was bad, too, because I had to ask Grandma about Hilliard House without her popping a vein. It needed to come up naturally, as part of a casual conversation. That meant letting Blake in on it, too.

I swallowed a bit of chili with corn bread and took a deep breath. "So . . . Grandma?"

"Are you meaning to ask me a question, Avery May?"

So much for *natural*.

"Yes, ma'am." I cleared my throat. "The other day when Julian Wayne and I were walking around the farm, he took an interest in that old Hilliard House. He wanted to know more about it, but I didn't know its history."

Grandma considered me for a moment. "You didn't take him near it, did you? You know I don't want anyone messing with that house."

Blake chuckled. "How could we forget after the stunt Avery pulled?"

Grandma's hard gaze didn't waver. "It's not safe. And it looks like I finally have a buyer to take it off my hands. The last thing I need is kids running around breaking things."

"He just wanted to know if it was built before the Civil War."

Grandma settled back in her chair and looked thoughtful. "I'm pretty sure Hilliard House was built after the Civil War." Her brow wrinkled. "There was a building in the same spot before that—a smaller frame house, I think, but it burned down."

"Did anyone die in the fire?" I asked.

"That's a gruesome question. I honestly don't know."

"Grandma, why didn't you and Grandpa live in Hilliard House?" Blake asked. "It's on your property. Seems like you'd want to live in a big house like that, looking out over the river and all."

Grandma put down her half-eaten corn stick. "It wasn't ours to live in."

Blake frowned. "Why not?"

"That's a long story."

"Can we hear it?" I prompted. "Please?"

"*May* you hear it, Avery May." She wiped her mouth. "The Hilliards have owned this land for a long time, but it didn't pass down as a whole from the first Hilliard to his first son, and then on to that Hilliard's first son. Instead, it was broken up into smaller bits, so that every son who wanted land got a parcel."

"What about the daughters?"

Blake rolled his eyes. "Girls don't inherit."

"That's not exactly true," said Grandma. "The girls just married men who had land of their own. Or they moved away, like your mother." Grandma's lips tightened. "Your grandpa's great-grandfather Ephraim Hilliard settled the area. It was his son, whose name I don't recall at the moment, who built that fancy brick house. *His* only surviving son, Joshua Hilliard, inherited the house. Your grandpa was his first cousin once removed, and they were neighbors."

"Why don't we have more cousins?" Blake asked. "You'd think this area would be chopped up into a hundred tiny farm parcels after that many generations."

"You're forgetting the wars, dear. Each one, from the Civil War to Vietnam, took at least one Hilliard boy, some of them not much older than you."

"So Joshua Hilliard was the last one to live in the brick house?" I asked.

"He was. I married your grandpa in 1960. Joshua Hilliard was around sixty-one at that time, already widowed and living alone in the house." She frowned. "He was a shut-in."

"Why?"

A shadow passed over Grandma's face, and for a moment I feared she might close down the whole conversation. But after letting out a heavy sigh, she continued.

"If you must know, Joshua Hilliard was a troubled man. He'd outlived his wife and daughter, and I reckon that's enough to make anyone maudlin."

"He's not still alive, though, right?"

"Good grief, Avery," Blake said. "He'd be, like, a hundred and fifty years old by now."

Grandma smiled. "Not quite. He died . . . I think it was around 1985." She looked past me toward the living room. "In his last years your grandpa collected all the old family photographs and organized them in albums. You might take a look at them."

"I'd like that." Actually, the idea of looking at black-and-white photos of frowning people in fusty clothes didn't exactly light my fire, but maybe it would help Julian with his film. "So nobody's lived in that house since? Even Grandpa didn't want it?"

"Your grandpa and I were happy here. And I never liked that house anyway."

"Why?" I asked.

"Old Joshua Hilliard wasn't just maudlin. There was a

darkness to him." She paused to scrape the last bite from her bowl. "Any more questions, my dear?"

I thought for a moment. "What does 'maudlin' mean?"

Blake leaned toward me. "It means feeling sorry for yourself. Which ought to sound familiar, since that's how you've been acting since we got here."

"Enough." Grandma settled her spoon in the empty bowl. "If you two clear the table, I'll bring in the watermelon. And, Blake, later on you can help Avery in the kitchen by drying the dishes."

It lifted my heart to see Blake getting punished for once. Too bad I didn't have much space in which to gloat about it while we were actually doing the dishes. It was hard to savor my triumph when he was standing next to me not saying anything. Turns out silence can actually be kind of loud and distracting.

So I passed the time by making a mental list of all his recent crimes against me. Things like telling me to walk behind him whenever we were in public, just in case some cute girl might mistake me for his girlfriend. Or not watching our favorite cartoon channel anymore because it was for "little kids."

Then there was the eye roll. That was a crime against Mom and Grandma, too. If any of us showed enthusiasm for anything—even important things—Blake gave us the eye roll. Sometimes it was big and dramatic, other times it was just a flicker, but it always burned me up. Just thinking about it was enough to make me want to break a plate.

"Come on, Avery, you're splashing me on purpose!"

I gave him a sidelong glance. His shirt *was* pretty damp, but I wasn't about to apologize.

"By the way, I remember something about Hilliard House," Blake said.

I rinsed a bowl and set it on the counter, even though his hand was outstretched to take it.

He sighed. "It came to me while you and Grandma were talking. It happened before you got yourself in trouble."

I set another bowl on the counter, willing my mask of boredom not to crack.

"We went over there together," he continued. "I was almost ten, so you must have been around seven years old. You wanted to go inside."

The mask cracked, and I turned to him. "I did?"

He grinned. "Yeah, you were fearless. The cellar door was open, and off you went crawling into the dark to find the steps up to the main floor."

"I don't remember that at all."

He dried a bowl and stacked it with the others. "It's been a long time. But you've always been weird about that house. First you were all obsessed, but after that walloping from Grandma, you stopped talking about it. Like you'd forgotten. Your face would go all blank when I mentioned it."

"Seriously?"

He nodded. "Sometime after that, when I thought you were with Grandma, I walked out there. As soon as I stepped on the porch, I heard something." He took another bowl from me, but this time he set it on the counter.

"Well . . . what'd you hear?" I prodded.

Blake made a display of side-eyeing the dishes, pans, and crusty Crock-Pot still waiting to be washed. "I'll tell you if you wash *and* dry the rest of this stuff."

My face flushed hot, and I could feel a vein start to throb at my temple. "You are the king of jerks."

He shrugged. "Whatever. It's up to you."

I stared at him, not even caring that my rubber gloves were dripping all over the floor. I wished I could forget the whole conversation, because I really wanted to see him dry the rest of those dishes.

But I wanted to know what he'd heard even more.

"Fine. I'll dry. Just tell me."

A slow smile spread across his face as he tossed the towel onto the counter. But when he turned back to me, the smile vanished.

"I heard *you*," he said. "I looked through the window and saw you sitting in a chair near the fireplace. You were talking to someone. I stared through that window really hard, looking all around that room to find who you were talking to."

I swallowed hard. "And?"

"And nothing. There was no one there but you."

That night I dreamed about Hilliard House.

I was walking up the hill toward the porch, and the brick-lined path seemed to extend about three times longer than I remembered. The grass between the bricks was dark and curled like worms. When I finally reached the steps, I raised my head to look at the house. A curtain twitched at the far-left window. A light glowed softly behind it, revealing the shadowy outline of a hand.

I woke to the shadows cast by my night-light. They stretched across the sloped attic walls, reaching out for me as if they were fingers, and the window air conditioner shuddered and wheezed like a creepy old chain-smoker. I fumbled at my bedside table until I finally switched on the lamp. At the bottom of the bed, Weasley lifted his head and mewed sleepily.

"It's okay, Wease. Go back to sleep."

I reached under the bed and pulled out the old coat box that lived there. It was dusty and more beat-up than I remembered, but I'd looked forward to opening it this summer . . . at least until Blake betrayed me.

I lifted the lid to find Kingdom nestled inside—the maps we'd made, the family trees, the battle plans and treaties, the stories and artwork, all detailing the adventures of Kingdom's inhabitants, from the mighty King Stanmore on his throne to the lowliest faun in his woodsy cottage. The pages were heavy in my lap, and they smelled like dust and kid sweat. But the stories and drawings chased the shadows away, and by the time I put the box back under the bed, I was ready to sleep.

CHAPTER 5

The next day I headed to Hollyhock Cottage right after lunch. Julian answered the door and waved me in. "Quick, let's go upstairs."

"Jules," said a voice from the kitchen. "Aren't you going to offer Miss Avery something to drink? A snack, maybe?"

Julian's shoulders slumped. "Dad won't leave me alone today," he murmured. "Go on in. If we give him what he wants, maybe he'll let us work."

The kitchen was warm and smelled like baking—sugar and vanilla. Curtis Wayne leaned on the counter near the sink, and he grinned when he saw me.

"Hey there, Avery May."

Nobody called me that but Grandma. Not even Mom. It brought a strange pang to my chest.

"Hi, Mr. Wayne."

"You want some iced tea? Lemonade? I made them myself."

Julian opened the fridge. "Dad, aren't you supposed to be *composing* or something?"

I glanced toward the living room and saw the guitar standing in exactly the same spot it had stood two days ago.

"I need to unwind a bit before the muse will strike," said Mr. Wayne. "And who's the dad here, anyway?"

I sort of wished I could freeze this moment and stare at Mr. Wayne without him knowing. It wasn't that I had a crush on him or anything. I mean, he was old. Like, *forty.* It's just . . . it was like looking at a cheetah in the zoo. Most dads I knew had bellies and gray hair and bags under their eyes. They were awkward around other people's kids, almost to the point of looking fearful. Most of all they just seemed weighed down by life. But here was a man about Mom's age standing in the kitchen in designer jeans, and not only did he look as sleek and relaxed as our cousin's prize-winning Racking Horse, he was baking cookies and *smiling* about it.

"What do you want, Avery?" Julian jerked his head out of the fridge. "Tea, lemonade, Michelob Ultra?"

"Very funny." Mr. Wayne quirked an eyebrow at me. "I trust you won't tell your grandmother that Julian has taken to offering alcohol to minors."

"I know better," I said. "She thinks drinking liquor is a sin. Her church uses grape juice for Communion."

Mr. Wayne nodded slowly. "I figured as much."

"I'll just have lemonade, please."

"Take some cookies, too." Mr. Wayne pulled a paper plate from the cabinet and scooped a couple of sugar cookies onto it.

Once we got to his room, Julian pulled the folding chair next to his leather office chair. "Sorry about that. He's really been hovering lately."

"He's not so bad."

"He disappears for weeks on tour, and then he comes

home and he's all clingy to make up for it. It's twice as bad here because this house is tiny and he's waiting for the muse, or whatever. He's probably baking a cake as we speak. Or making cucumber sandwiches. I bet your dad isn't like that. Am I right?"

I froze. All these years of having a prepared answer to the dad question and I completely locked up.

"Avery?"

"My dad," I finally said, keeping my face still and sad, "is dead."

Julian choked on a bite of cookie. "Sorry," he said, brushing crumbs off his mouth. "I had no idea."

"I don't like to talk about it."

"Yeah, I get it." He took a long swallow of lemonade and cleared his throat. "So, what did you learn about Hilliard House?"

This was one thing I liked about boys—you could always count on them to change the subject if *feelings* came up. I told him everything Grandma had said, such as when the house was built, and how the last owner outlived his wife and daughter.

Julian nodded. "An old recluse, huh? Anything else?"

Oh, and I used to visit an imaginary friend in that house.

"Not really," was what I actually said.

"Do you know how his wife and child died? Anything interesting about that?"

"Grandma didn't say. I don't think she knows."

"We need to do more research, but Dad took my smartphone and there's no Wi-Fi in this house."

"Why'd he take your phone?"

Julian looked away. "Supposedly I spend too much time on the Internet. He said I had to take a break while we're here. It's lame, I know."

"Well, you wouldn't get good reception up here anyway. Blake sure doesn't. And if you need to do research, there's a shelf of books on local history downstairs. Grandma always keeps stuff like that for tourists. But, Julian, I don't see why it matters what happened to his family. Aren't we just making up the story ourselves?"

His eyes widened. "With a setting like this, I want to use as much of the local lore as possible. It'll add authenticity to our film, and that sort of thing is great for marketing."

"Marketing?"

"Yeah, once it's finished we could build a whole website around it, and the connection to local history might draw more traffic."

It had never occurred to me that anyone other than us might see this film. It'd just seemed like a good summer project for friends, something to pass the time, but Julian made it sound like a business opportunity.

"If you can't find what you need in those books, we could try the library," I said. "It's about thirty minutes away by car—I could ask Grandma to drive us."

"Nothing in walking distance?"

"In case you hadn't noticed, everything's pretty spread out around here."

Julian frowned. "What about that graveyard just down the road? You can learn a lot from gravestones, plus we could get some good footage for our film. Are all the Hilliards buried there?"

"Just the dead ones." I grinned. "And Grandma won't mind us walking down there."

"Maybe we could do that Wednesday."

"Are we writing the script today?"

He gave me a sidelong look. "You have a lot of work to do before we start that."

"*Work?* What kind of work?"

"I want to take advantage of the creepy qualities of Hilliard House. Have you ever watched a scary movie?"

I flinched. "Wait a minute . . . are *we* making a scary movie?"

Julian leaned forward in his chair. "Did something bad happen to you at that house? Other than your grandmother taking a belt to you?"

I thought of last night's dream. The hand in the window.

"All I know is that house creeps me out."

"This is just a movie, Avery. It's no big deal. Just think of it as pretending."

I took a breath. "Okay."

"So . . . what scary movies have you watched?"

I thought for a moment. "One time Blake and I watched this old movie called *Excalibur*. It was edited for TV, but there was still a lot of blood. Like, spears poking in people's guts with blood spurting out, and crows eating the eyeballs out of a dead guy's head. It was super gross."

He shook his head. "That's just gore. Have you ever watched a *ghost* movie?"

"Definitely not. Mom hates ghost stories, and Grandma only watches *Little House on the Prairie* and old stuff like that."

"Yeah, you definitely have some catching up to do." When

I started to protest, he lifted a hand. "The good news is that I'll do the work with you right here. It'll be a good review for me, and I bet we'll get all sorts of ideas for our own story."

"Um, I didn't come here to sign up for summer school."

"I promise you'll like this, Avery."

I rolled my eyes. But doing that made me think of Blake and how he never wanted to do anything fun anymore.

"All right, then. Bring on the ghost movies."

Julian smiled. "We'll start with a classic."

CHAPTER 6

Julian kept a warehouse's worth of movies on his external hard drive, so we watched on the jumbo monitor with the lights off and curtains closed. His dad insisted the door stay open, but even then not much light came from the hallway. Julian reclined in his leather chair with his feet propped up on a box, and I sat on the bed because he told me to. Blake's bed was a jumble of covers and smelled like feet, but Julian's was smooth and tucked in, and all I smelled was clean cotton.

I worried at first because I had a strict policy about black-and-white movies. It mostly involved *never* watching them. In old movies, everybody talked in funny, false-sounding voices, and the story moved about as fast as molasses. I'd tried many times to watch *It's a Wonderful Life* at Christmas—Mom really loved it—but I always fell asleep in the first twenty minutes. And that was on a *couch,* not a comfy bed like Julian's.

This movie was different.

It started with an old-fashioned voice-over in which a man told the story of a very bad house and the people who'd died in it. Years later, a group of strangers arrived at the house to study paranormal activity. Everything seemed fine in the light of day, but when they went to bed . . . that's when the creepy stuff started happening. Strange poundings and crying noises echoed through the halls at night. Doorknobs rattled and the doors themselves seemed to breathe in and out.

At one point I had to ask Julian to pause it. I said I needed a bathroom break, but really, I just had to get away from that crazy house for a second. It was getting too real. I needed to see sunlight coming through the bathroom window and to hear Julian's dad puttering downstairs in the kitchen.

When the movie was over, my shoulders finally relaxed. It was a relief to turn the lights on, to stretch and yawn.

Julian studied me. "Were you scared?"

"Yeah . . . I guess."

"Why?"

"I don't know. I just was."

He sighed. "If you're going to be serious about film-making, you need to figure out *why* it was scary."

I thought so long and hard that the silence rang in my ears and my armpits turned sweaty.

"Was it the violence that scared you?" he prompted.

I snorted. "There wasn't any. No blood, anyway."

"Was it the ghost?"

"Well, *yeah!*"

"Was it the way the ghost looked?"

I started to say yes, but stopped. We'd heard horrible thumps and cries. We saw what seemed to be the ghost turning the doorknob and pressing against the door itself. But I didn't know what the ghost looked like.

"We never actually saw it," I said.

"So why was the movie scary?"

"Because I didn't know what the ghost was. It seemed dangerous, but I didn't know what it would do. I was just . . . *dreading* it the whole time."

Julian nodded. "Psychological horror. The unknown is much scarier than a vampire, or a werewolf, or a man in a sheet yelling 'boo.'"

"I'd never be scared by a man in a sheet."

"You know what I mean."

We watched the movie again, but this time it was easier because I knew what to expect. In fact, the scary bits were almost fun because I could study how they scared me.

The coolest thing was when Julian paused the movie to explain camera angles. He showed me how a low angle, where the camera is placed below the subject, makes that person or thing seem powerful and intimidating. The director of this movie used low angles a *lot*, like when the characters first saw the house and it stood dark and gloomy above them. High angles made people or things look insignificant. When the characters were frightened in this movie, they were shown from high angles. It made them look small and powerless. And when the camera tilted or shook? That helped you feel a character's loss of control or fear.

"I always thought the most important thing was the acting. I never realized how much work the camera actually does in telling the story." I shook my head in wonder. "How do you know all this stuff?"

"I did a camp last summer. One of the tracks was filmmaking, and the teacher was totally into classic horror films. I guess I got a little obsessed."

"Julian, who's going to star in our movie?"

"*We* are, of course. And maybe my sister. Do you think your brother would be interested?"

"I seriously doubt it." It was time to move the subject as far from Blake as possible, so I pointed toward the computer. "I just wondered if our movie would be about grown-ups or kids. I mean—will you have *us* playing grown-ups?"

"No way. Things have to feel real. If we had funding, we could hire actors, but our characters need to be kids because we basically have no budget." His eyes brightened. "That's another good thing about psychological horror. If you never show the ghost, you don't need a huge budget for special effects."

"Hadn't thought of that."

"And it's better anyway. My film teacher said that creepy monsters jumping out at you from the screen might make you scream, but it's the things you *don't* see that really get under your skin."

A knock came at the door, and I swear my body rose about a foot off the bed. But it was only Julian's dad poking his head in. He held a cell phone in his hand.

"Avery May, your grandma just called. She says it's time to get ready for supper."

I glanced at my watch. "I've been here for almost five hours. How did that happen?"

Mr. Wayne just smiled. "Better get a move on."

That night when Mom called, my brain was bursting with everything I'd seen and learned at Hollyhock Cottage. I'd been thinking a lot about that haunted-house movie, and part of me really wanted to talk to Mom about it. But if I did, I'd have to explain how Julian and I were making a ghost movie of our own. And since she wouldn't even let me *watch* a ghost movie, I was pretty sure she wouldn't be happy about us making one.

"You sound kind of far away tonight, Avery," she said.

"I'm just tired, I guess."

"Are you and Blake running around all day like always?"

"Me and *who*?"

There was a pause. "Avery?"

"I barely speak to Blake anymore, Mom."

"But I thought you had a royal wedding to arrange for Kingdom. Princess . . . what was her name?"

"Etheline. She was supposed to marry the Lord of the North Countries, but Blake thinks he's too old to play anymore. He says he's starting *high school*. Kingdom is *little kid stuff*. I got in big trouble with Grandma for cussing at him, but he was asking for it."

"Oh, Avery, I wish you'd get a handle on that temper of yours. Next time he makes you mad, count to five in your head before you talk back to him. Will you try that, please?"

I couldn't think of any time in my life when *counting* had calmed me down, but if I said that Mom would think I was sassing her. "Yes, ma'am."

She took a breath. "And anyway, Grandma says you've made a new friend already. One of her summer tenants?"

"It's just Julian. We're making a film together."

"How ambitious."

She was using that "playing along" tone that always irked

me, especially because I was almost sure she'd just held the phone away from her mouth to yawn.

"Actually, we're making a film about the Hilliard farm."

"That sounds interesting."

Sometimes she'd be on her computer at the same time she was talking to me, checking work email, and I'd only get half of her attention.

"Yeah, we're flying in actors from Hollywood," I said. "Julian is a famous teen director."

"Uh-huh . . ."

Now I knew she wasn't listening. "Tomorrow we start filming the nude scenes."

"Right."

"Mom! I just said we were filming *nude scenes*. Are you on the computer or something?"

"Oh, honey, I'm sorry." She cleared her throat. "My brain's a bit scrambled after the long day. I've been putting in extra hours at work, trying to get ahead on some of these cases so I won't be distracted when I fly out there to see you."

"You're always distracted."

"I'm trying to get on top of all this, honey. I really am."

"I know," I whispered.

CHAPTER 7

It took Julian a little while to come to the door Tuesday morning, and this time no sweet smells of baking greeted me in the hallway. Instead I heard the guitar strumming in the living room.

"Dad is *finally* composing, so he'll leave us alone," Julian whispered, waving me toward the stairs.

"Can we stand here and listen for a bit?"

"No time to waste. We've got two more movies to watch before filming starts."

"But I've never heard anyone write a song before."

Julian frowned. "What do you want to be, Avery? A groupie or a filmmaker?"

"Geez, I was just curious."

Once we'd settled ourselves in his room—Julian stiff and serious in his leather chair and me perched on the bed—he leaned forward. "I've decided our film should be black and white."

For some reason I thought of those old cameras you saw in movies, the kind you had to wind as you filmed. I couldn't really see Julian doing that. "You mean on actual black-and-white film?"

"I wish. I don't even know how to use a camera with actual film. I learned on a digital camera, and that's what we'll be using. We can change it to black and white afterwards. I have all sorts of cool filters we can use in postproduction."

Julian had queued up the movie as he was talking, and this one was about a lady who was taking care of two little children in a beautiful mansion long ago. The creepy music during the opening credits probably should have clued me in, but it was still strange to see that sweet little boy and girl turn weird on her. And when the ghosts started to peek through windows and appear on the towers? The hair lifted on the back of my neck. But I didn't let it get to me. Not *really*. Things that would have made me shut my eyes only a few days ago didn't bother me so much now, and I think it was because I was *studying* the movie.

Here's what I noticed: this movie had a lot more close-ups than the last one. In the other movie, the shots were so wide that you saw a lot of the house—the furniture and wallpaper and stuff—and the character would be a small, helpless thing at the center of the screen. That made sense to me, because in that movie the house was the bad guy, and the characters were in its clutches. In this movie, a character's face would fill the entire screen. It was almost claustrophobic, and I was proud of myself for thinking of that word when I explained my thoughts to Julian.

"That's a good way to describe it," he said. "The shots are so tight it's like there's no room to breathe. But how does it fit the story? Is there anything about *her* that makes you feel kind of, um . . ."

"Kind of what?" I asked.

"Smothered?"

His face was a little strange when he asked that—almost like he was trying not to flinch or something. I got the sense that he'd clam right up if I asked him about it, so I took a moment to ponder the question.

"I think the close-ups are important because . . . well, we see everything from her point of view. She's the first one who decides there are ghosts. She's the one who decides the little boy is bad. By the end, it's almost like she made the whole thing up."

Julian smiled. "Good work, Avery. You've picked up film analysis quicker than I thought you might." He turned to pull something out of a box on his desk. "I'm loaning you my tablet. I added the last ghost film for you to watch tonight— that way we can get to the filming faster."

I took the tablet and tried to imagine watching a spooky movie in the attic with the air conditioner wheezing and the shadows reaching for me.

"And, Avery?" Julian said. "Try to get that key soon. To- morrow we'll find some cool stuff at the cemetery, and then it's on to Hilliard House."

Later that evening, after I'd said good night to Grandma, I set up Julian's tablet at the end of my bed. He'd showed me where to find the ghost movie and how to play it, but first I wanted to see what else he had. It was pretty nosy of me, but I figured he wouldn't give me the tablet if there was some- thing super private on it.

He had the usual Internet and social networking apps, but

since it was a Wi-Fi tablet, there was no point in opening those. His photos and videos were recent ones of the farm and Hilliard House. Nothing from before I met him except for a five-second clip filmed in a noisy school lunchroom titled "Bullied3." It was just a shaky view of kids sitting at a table, so I figured it was something old he'd forgotten to delete.

The only other thing that caught my eye was an app called "Media Vault," which I recognized because Blake had installed it on his phone once. That had only lasted a day, though. The instant Mom saw it she forced him to take it off, because it was for hiding photos and videos you didn't want anyone else to see. Knowing Blake, he'd probably put his own selfies in there or something sad like that. What would Julian hide? When I clicked the app, it prompted me for a password, just as I'd expected. I didn't bother to type anything—I was already yawning my head off, so there was no way I'd crack Julian's code tonight.

Since there was nothing else to snoop through, I turned the air conditioner down and opened the movie Julian had told me to watch. The opening credits dragged on for about a hundred years, and I had to turn the volume down because the music was loud and dramatic in that "HARK, A SCARY MOVIE!" way.

Finally the story started with a man and a woman finding a beautiful old house on a cliff that faced the sea. They talked really fast in that old-fashioned, prissy style that annoyed me about black-and-white movies. I'd been worried this one would be too creepy for me to watch alone in the attic, but it was so old-timey that it didn't get under my skin at all. When the man and woman turned out to be brother and sister—and bought the house so they could live there *together*—I gave up and crawled under the covers.

My second-to-last thought before I fell asleep was that Blake would have found the whole brother-and-sister thing hilarious. My last thought was that he would never know because there was no way I was going to tell him about it.

CHAPTER 8

The next day Julian and I took the gravel road down to the blacktopped highway that led to Clearview Cemetery. The sky was bright blue and a light breeze carried the scent of freshly mown grass. I waited quietly as Julian took in the flowers on the headstones and the tall trees that leaned forward to make a curtain around the graves.

"Huh," he said. "It's like a park. Only with dead people." He turned to me. "Is your dad's grave here?"

My stomach convulsed. He'd caught me off guard *again*. "Um, no."

"Why not?"

Why, why, why? The answers came so easy to me back home, but here . . . somehow it was harder to lie. "Because he wasn't from around here."

That much *was* true.

Julian nodded. "I know you don't like talking about him. I just wanted to pay my respects if his grave was here."

The tightness in my shoulders eased up. Sometimes he talked like he was a lot older—maybe it was all those old movies he watched—but that was the most gentlemanly thing I'd heard him say. Heck, it was the most gentlemanly thing I'd heard *anyone* say.

I grinned. "Are you hungry? Because I worked all morning in the garden and now I'm starving. Plus, I want to show you something."

A wooden fence lay on the eastern edge of the cemetery, and on the other side was a wooded area. Within those woods was a grove of dwarf blue spruce trees. When we were younger, Blake and I decided the grove was a magical place. A forest within a forest, blue within green. It was quiet and cool there, the perfect spot for spinning tales about Kingdom during the hottest part of the day.

I climbed over the fence and looked back at Julian. "Coming?"

"Will I be trespassing again?"

"The land across the fence belongs to Mr. Shepherd, but he's never shot at us or anything."

Julian froze and looked around, as if expecting a crazy rifleman to appear from the tree line.

"It's safe, I promise." As soon as he was on my side of the fence, I led him to the circle of plump spruce trees. Then I handed him a sandwich and water bottle from my knapsack. "This is the secret grove. Cool, huh?"

"Do you and your brother come here a lot?"

"We used to."

He raised an eyebrow. "Not anymore?"

"He's changed," I said flatly. "Actually, more like *mutated.*"

"Into . . . ?"

"A jerk."

Julian twisted the cap off his water and took a swig. "I was an only child for a long time. I always wanted a brother. Then Lily came along."

I couldn't read his face. "Did you love her or hate her?"

"I didn't feel anything at first. All babies do is cry and drool and stink. One time Dad made me change her dirty diaper, and I threw up."

"Gross!"

"When she finally started using the potty, and when we could actually talk to each other, I liked her better." He took the sandwich out of the baggie and sniffed it. "Is this ham and Swiss?"

I nodded. "When is Lily coming?"

"Very soon," he said. "So what'd you think of that movie I told you to watch?"

I swallowed a gulp of water. "Actually, I fell asleep. It started out kind of slow, and I was really tired."

"Can you watch it tonight? I promise the story picks up once they move into the house."

"It's a lot easier when we watch during the day on your big screen."

"Fine," he said. "But it'll put us a day behind. Did you at least get the key?"

"Not yet, but I *will*."

As soon as we'd put away the lunch stuff, I took him to Grandma and Grandpa's plot. I'd never taken the time to find all the Hilliard graves before, but this seemed like the best place to start. It was a wide headstone inscribed with a verse from the book of John:

I AM THE RESURRECTION, AND THE LIFE; HE THAT BELIEVETH
IN ME, THOUGH HE WERE DEAD, YET SHALL HE LIVE.

"'Samuel Hilliard,'" Julian read. "'Born March 26, 1935, died August 7, 2002.'"

"My grandpa."

"He wasn't that old, was he?"

"Heart disease. Grandma said he hated going to the doctor." I swatted at a buzzing bee. "She still talks to him whenever we come by to tidy the grave. She likes to fill him in on the latest news."

Julian pointed at the headstone where Grandma's name—Ava Louise—was already etched in along with her birth date. "Does everyone do that?" he asked. "Put their name on the stone before they've even died?"

"A lot of them do. I mean, if you're married, you go ahead and buy the plot for two people." I shivered. "I wouldn't want to see *my* name on a gravestone, though."

Julian traced Grandma's birth year with his finger. "Can you imagine your grandmother visiting this grave and seeing a *death* date chiseled on her side? And that's when she realizes she's a ghost? That would be a cool scene in a movie." He pulled a small notebook and pen out of his pocket and scribbled.

After that we wandered around the headstones, looking for more Hilliards. Near a knotty tree I found a collection of old headstones, thinner and lower to the ground than the newer ones. Julian stood at my side as I bent down to peer at the inscriptions.

"This green mold makes it harder to read the words," I said.

"It's lichen, actually." He reached for his camera. "And it looks great on film, but I'm not sure how it will translate to black and white. . . ."

He was totally absorbed in taking close-up shots of the moldy lettering, so I studied the other Hilliard headstones. "Hey, this Ephraim guy was the one who settled Grandma's land." I stepped toward the neighboring headstone. "And this must be his son Josiah—the one who actually built Hilliard House. Grandma couldn't remember his name the other day, but the dates look right."

Julian had already moved on to study the next row of headstones. "Who was it that outlived his family?" he asked. "You know, the last Hilliard to live in that house?"

"Joshua. But he died in the eighties—he's probably farther back in the cemetery."

"I think I've found him. Come here."

He stood midway between two headstones and pointed to the one on his right. "This is him, right?"

JOSHUA EVERETT HILLIARD
AUGUST 23, 1899–FEBRUARY 5, 1985

It was the plainest of headstones, thick but not very wide. No carvings or quotations from the Bible. Just his name and dates engraved in stark lettering.

"There's another stone over there," Julian said. "It's what I really wanted you to see."

I followed him to a wide stone of thick, expensive granite. It had two names on it.

ELIZABETH ANNE CUNNINGHAM HILLIARD

NOVEMBER 10, 1905–APRIL 10, 1955

MARGARET ANNE HILLIARD

JANUARY 5, 1930–FEBRUARY 12, 1937

Julian glanced at me. "It's interesting, isn't it?"

"Mother and daughter?"

"Yeah, and I bet Elizabeth was Joshua's wife. Can you check with your grandma?"

I nodded slowly. "Poor little Margaret. Only seven years old when she died. And when they buried her, they left room for the mom but not the dad. What's up with that?"

"It is a bit peculiar." Julian took several close-up shots of the headstone. "Yesterday I checked that shelf of local history books at your grandma's cottage. I found an old paperback about the Carver County floods of 1937. The big flood in February was the worst—houses were swept away and people died."

"Yeah, so?"

"Avery, look at the death date on Margaret Anne's grave." His eyes gleamed as he pointed at the stone. "1937. *February* 1937. I bet she drowned in the flood. And you know what that means?"

I shook my head.

"Our film has its ghost."

CHAPTER 9

I stared at the ceiling for quite a while that night, thinking about this so-called ghost Julian had in mind for our movie. To say I didn't feel so great about the idea was what Blake would call a "massive understatement." But had I said anything to Julian?

Of course not.

He'd had that lively look in his eyes again—that creative spark that seemed to light me up, too. Truth was, while I was sitting next to him, I almost thought I could handle a spooky movie with a ghost. Even at *Hilliard House*. As Julian said, we were just telling stories. It was all pretend, right?

But in the darkness of the attic, with only the faint yellow glow of my night-light to keep me company, it wasn't so simple. I just didn't know how to explain that to Julian.

He answered the door the next day, and once again there wasn't a whiff of baking in the air. I hoped Curtis Wayne might say "hey" from the living room, but he didn't even look up from his guitar. The tune he was strumming sounded angry, and I couldn't help noticing the patchy gray scruff on his cheeks and the way his hair was mashed on one side of his head.

"The desperate and unshowered phase," Julian murmured.

Once we were settled in his room, he queued up the movie I'd started two nights before.

"Lily was supposed to come last night," he said, "but the driver is bringing her tonight instead. So we're not as much behind schedule as I thought. Are you going to bring my tablet back?"

"Yeah. I just forgot." I flinched as the opening credits blared. "That music is freaking annoying."

"This is the last one we're watching," he said. "It's also the oldest of the three and the most traditional haunted house story. That's why I wanted you to see it."

I watched again as the brother and sister explored the house that overlooked the sea—a house that turned out to be haunted, of course. But their story ended a little different from the others because the characters actually tried to communicate with the ghost through a séance. For a movie that started out kind of silly, that scene made my scalp prickle. And when the ghost actually appeared? The prickles snaked all the way down my spine. By the time the siblings figured everything out and saved the day, I decided the movie wasn't half bad.

"So . . ." Julian stretched his shoulders. "I'm not going to ask if you liked it. I just want to know what you found interesting from a filmmaking perspective."

My chest swelled a little at the idea of myself as a *filmmaker*. "Well, it was another movie about a big old house that's haunted. And we got to see the ghost."

"What else?"

"Um, since everyone saw the ghost, you knew it was really there. You couldn't say, 'That's the main character's imagination.'" I knew that was right, and it made my heart beat a little faster. "The ghost was pretty cool, too. It wasn't a person in a sheet, or wearing spooky makeup. It was just a wisp floating around, but it gave me chills." I thought for a moment. "Can you create something like that on your computer?"

Julian pursed his mouth before answering. "Maybe. And I agree that the subtle special effects were good in this movie. But was it the wispy thing that scared you or something else?"

"I guess it was the character's reactions."

He slapped his hand on the desk, making me jump.

"That's what I'm talking about. We may not be able to create special effects, but we can show our 'ghost' in a different way."

"We can show how scary it is by our reaction to it."

He smiled. "I think we'll be ready to start making this movie soon. But you know what we need first?"

"I know, I know." Panic knotted in my stomach. "We need the key to Hilliard House."

Grandma kept the keys to her properties in her bedroom—*not* an easy place to sneak in and out of. Good thing she kept her shrine to Grandpa there, too. The shelves opposite her and Grandpa's twin beds were filled with his favorite books, including the albums that held family photos dating back to when cameras were first invented. I'd already told Grandma I wanted to look at old photos, so I hoped she wouldn't be too suspicious when I asked to hang out in her room and flip through them.

"Those albums were your grandpa's final achievement," she said. "He wasn't as spry as he'd once been, but he was determined to get those boxes of old photos properly arranged in albums before he . . ." Grandma swallowed the rest of the sentence and reached out to stroke the gold-stamped design on one of the album spines. "You'll be careful, won't you? Only take down one album at a time."

"I know, Grandma."

Weasley announced his arrival with a low trill, halfway between a meow and a purr, and leapt into the middle of Grandpa's bed. He was the only creature other than Mom allowed that privilege, and he rubbed it in by rolling on his back and noisily grooming his belly.

I pulled the first album from the shelf and carried it with two hands to Grandma's bed. "Is it okay if I sit here?"

She nodded. "I'll be watching TV in the living room if you need me."

I sat there holding the album until I heard the first notes of the *Little House on the Prairie* theme song. Then I set the album on the bed and tiptoed to her key drawer.

I eased it open as quietly as possible. Inside was a plastic tray divided into sections for organizing small things. Grandma put all her keys in there—ones for the houses, the car, the old tractor, the outbuildings, and even a small one for a bank vault. I picked through the round, metal-edged tags until I found the one for Hilliard House. I'd kind of expected an old-timey key, something heavy with a fancy handle, but it was just a plain dead-bolt key.

I slipped it into my pocket and put one of the extra out-building keys in its spot. If you didn't look too hard, you might think it was the Hilliard House key. I closed the drawer without making a sound.

"What are you doing, Avery?"

My heart lurched in my chest. I whipped my head around to see Blake in the doorway.

CHAPTER 10

He stepped just inside the door. "Why are you messing with Grandma's keys? She'd probably want to know. Should I call her in here?"

Blake's eyes gleamed. I guess catching me in the act of stealing was enough to finally wipe that bored look off his face.

I stared him down. "Go ahead, jerkface."

"All right, then." He grinned and turned to go.

"No, wait." I sighed. "What do I have to do?"

"First tell me why you took that key."

Various lies flashed through my brain, but they were all pretty weak. Blake could be a tool, but he wasn't *stupid,* so my best option was to keep it simple and honest. "Julian and I are making a movie, and he wants to film inside the old Hilliard House."

He blinked. "You're making a movie?" After staring at me for a moment, he shook his head. "Grandma told you never to go in that house again, and I don't blame her. Something spooky was going on there."

"I don't remember any of that. I just want to make this

movie." I crossed my arms. "What do I have to do to keep you from telling?"

He pretended to consider this carefully, but I knew what was coming.

"You have to do the crappy garden stuff this summer. Weeding. Okra picking. Potatoes. I'll do beans, lettuce, cantaloupes, and watermelon."

"Fine," I said quickly.

"Hold up! Did you think that was it?" He leaned against the doorframe. "You also have to shell all the peas. I'll snap the beans."

"That's not fair," I blurted. "Shelling is a lot harder. And we always split the chores down the middle."

"That was before you took up a life of crime." He gestured toward the living room. "Confess to her right now and you're free. You'll just have to deal with her punishment. Mom's, too, when she gets here. You may not get to do the movie at all."

I stared back at him, feeling like the biggest dope on the planet. Blake hadn't used his brain more than twice since we got here, but at the first whiff of a blackmail scheme he'd morphed into a freaking mastermind.

"Is it a deal, Avery?"

I sighed. "Deal."

He didn't move.

"Now what?" I asked.

"I'm supposed to ask if you want some watermelon."

"Leave me a couple of slices on the kitchen table."

As soon as Blake hauled his smug face out of Grandma's

bedroom, I shot a dirty look at Weasley. "You could have warned me he was coming."

The cat blinked. Then his mouth opened wide in a yawn.

"Yeah, I see whose side you're on."

I glanced back at the album lying on Grandma's bed. If I put it away and left now, she would know I hadn't spent much time with Grandpa's precious photographs. So I sat down and pulled the heavy thing back in my lap. The album was the old-fashioned kind with sticky pages and a plastic sheet for protecting the photos. The pages were starting to yellow, and some of the photos had already shifted a little.

The first few pages held photographs that were really, truly old, and some of them looked like they were made of glass or metal. The people in them seemed tired and thin, with weathered skin and lips pressed into thin lines. Their eyes stared.

Grandpa had labeled all the photographs, so it looked like I would have a face for each of the Hilliard men Grandma had mentioned last Sunday. In one faded photo, Ephraim Hilliard sat in front of the house, and he must have been pretty old because his hair was nearly gone and his face looked like a shriveled nut. His son Josiah stood behind him. They both wore their church clothes—jackets with handkerchiefs in the pockets, vests buttoned up all the way with dark ties tucked inside. They looked uncomfortable, and I bet they changed into their farming clothes as soon as the camera was packed away.

The women had hair parted in the middle and slicked back in tight buns. As time went on, the hair of the Hilliard ladies got rounder and poofier. In one photo from the early

1900s, my great-great-grandma Clemie stared from beneath a head of hair about as wide as a pumpkin. Her grim face told me she'd lived through at least thirty years of hardship, but according to Grandpa's note she was only fourteen.

My heart thumped a little faster when I found Joshua Hilliard, the last person to live in Hilliard House. He appeared in a couple of group photographs as a small child, sulky-looking with long hair and wearing a white gown instead of shirt and pants. A couple of pages later I found a portrait of him all grown up and in uniform. Grandma had said the Hilliard boys always went to war, and Joshua was no different. I'd seen a TV show about the First World War, so I knew he'd probably spent a lot of time sitting in a rat-infested trench, watching the skies for artillery and mustard gas. All while waiting for the call to climb out and get shot at.

But he survived, of course, and married Elizabeth Anne Cunningham. In their wedding portrait he looked pretty slick in a pin-striped suit, and Elizabeth Anne was sweet with her curly golden bob. She didn't wear a veil, but her ankle-length white dress had pearls sewn all over it. I studied that photograph for quite a while. They seemed so happy. It made me sad to think of them buried under different headstones, separated forever in death.

After that, the photos shifted to Grandpa's father and mother, and I thought maybe he never had any photos of Joshua Hilliard's daughter. Then I came across another group shot taken in front of Hilliard House, probably at Thanksgiving because the trees were looking bare and the women wore shawls and light coats. The men stood, the women sat in chairs before them, and the children sat on the ground.

I found Elizabeth Anne first. She was still bright-eyed and beautiful. Nestled at her feet was a very slight girl with white-blond hair that fluffed around her head like a dandelion about to blow its seeds. The other kids looked at the camera, as they'd likely been told, but her head was turned as if she was distracted by something in the distance.

Grandpa had dated the photograph 1935. Margaret Anne was five years old.

In about fourteen months she would be dead.

I shook my head and reached for the next album, which mostly had photos of Grandpa when he was a little boy. The album after that had photos of Grandpa and Grandma sitting together and smiling, holding hands—what Grandma called "courting"—and then getting married, working the farm. Once Grandpa took over the farm, he stopped smiling.

Finally, in the last few pages, there were photos of Mom.

I giggled at the baby pictures of her toothless grin and bald head. I'd seen copies of them in Mom's scrapbooks. Once she was walking, the photos turned to color: Mom on her first day of school, wearing a patchwork dress that flared out around her knees, her hair in bushy pigtails; Mom in skirts with kneesocks; Mom in church clothes with a bow on her head, standing next to Grandma. I stared at that last photo, wondering if there were other kids at Sycamore Road Church of Christ in those days. Mom didn't talk much about that time except to complain about her loneliness and Grandpa's strict rules.

There was one shot of Mom in a plaid shirt and overalls, sitting with Grandpa on the tractor, but otherwise it was all dresses and skirts. Mom told me she fought the family dress code once she got to high school, and I guess Grandma lost the battle. The later photos were inserted just as carefully as all of the others, but I could feel Grandpa's disapproval clinging to the shots of Mom in jeans, Mom wearing eye shadow and lipstick.

"Avery May, your watermelon's waiting," Grandma called from the living room. "Everything all right in there?"

"Yes, ma'am," I said. "Almost done."

Once Mom graduated from high school, the photos nearly stopped altogether. The very last one showed her sitting on the porch swing in 1987. Her hair was pulled back in a huge white scrunchie, and she was wearing a dress again. She had a tan, and her cheeks were pink from too much sun. Excitement flashed in her eyes.

When I looked closer, I noticed that her right hand was holding something. Someone else's hand. In fact, the photo had been folded under to cover that person up.

The *Little House* closing credits were blaring in the living room, but I still took care to peel the plastic very slowly so Grandma wouldn't hear the ripping sound. Loosening each corner carefully, I pulled the photograph away from the sticky backing. Then I unfolded it.

Sitting next to Mom, holding her hand, was a young man with light brown hair.

She was looking at the camera, but he was looking at her. An old boyfriend? I studied their clasped hands. She had a band on her ring finger. I squinted at his left hand. There was a thin gold band on his ring finger, too.

I didn't know this man. In fact, I'd never seen him before in my life.

CHAPTER 11

I told people my father was dead because the truth was too weird.

When people asked Blake, he looked them straight in the eye and said, "I don't have a dad." Somehow he got away with that. Nobody ever asked for more details. Mom would say, "Their father is not in the picture," and people would nod their heads and change the subject.

I told people my dad was dead and it hurt too much to talk about him. My teachers hardly ever brought it up, probably because Mom had already dropped her line on them during enrollment or conferences. My friends never pressed for details. I guess having a dead dad wasn't a big deal in the big city of Dallas, where some kids had two dads or two moms or lived with their grandparents or were adopted from China.

I was mostly okay . . . until someone like Julian—with his cookie-baking, million-dollar smile, superstar dad—threw me for a loop by asking about it.

Or until I saw a photo like the one I'd just stolen from Grandpa's album.

I slipped the folded photo in my back pocket and joined

Grandma in the living room. She'd started another episode of *Little House*—the one in which Pa finds Mr. Edwards drunk and brawling in a saloon—so I stood next to the couch and waited for the scene break.

Grandma lifted her clunky remote to pause the tape. "Find anything interesting in those albums?"

I nodded. "Lots of stuff. Grandpa did a nice job putting it all together and labeling everything." I shifted my weight from one foot to the other, trying to think of something to say that didn't sound fake. "I used to think old photos were boring, but when it's your family . . . it can be kinda cool."

Grandma's mouth quirked. "True enough." She glanced at the wall clock. "You better get to that watermelon before it's time for bed."

"First I need to ask Blake something real quick."

"Well, don't just barge in there, Avery May. Knock politely and wait to be invited in."

"Yes, ma'am."

When Blake and I first came to stay with Grandma in Tennessee, we'd shared bunk beds in the attic. Two years ago he'd moved to Grandpa's old music room, which was connected to the main house by a breezeway. It wasn't as cool as the attic, but it was almost as private and had Grandpa's beautiful old mandolins hanging on the wall. Plus it was a lot closer to the bathroom.

I tapped on Blake's door. "It's just me. I gotta ask you something urgent."

"It's not locked."

He was sprawled on the bed staring at a *Texas Football*

magazine. One of the books from his summer-reading list sat next to him with a scrap of paper marking his progress. He hadn't made much.

I waited for him to look up.

He turned a page.

I cleared my throat.

"There will be no renegotiation," he said, still staring at the magazine.

I pulled the photograph out of my pocket. "I need to show you something."

When he finally looked up, I handed it to him.

He studied the photo and shrugged. "It's Mom and some guy."

"They're holding hands. Notice any interesting jewelry on their fingers?"

He looked closer. "Oh."

"Mom was married, Blake. You know what this means? She might have lied to us." I tapped the photo. "*He* could be our—"

"He's not."

"What?"

Blake raised his head, his eyes meeting mine. "He's not our dad. That's what you were going to say, wasn't it?"

"How do you know?"

He handed the photo back to me. "Mom was married, but it only lasted a year. I was born a decade later."

My mouth fell open, but my brain couldn't seem to push any words out. Blake already *knew*. He must have known for a long time.

"Mom told you about this? She told *you* and not me?"

"She was waiting to tell you because . . . well, you tend to . . ."

I could feel the blood pounding in my temples. "I tend to *what?*"

"Go nuclear." He put his fists together and exploded the fingers outward. "I guess she was waiting until you were older and could, you know, handle the truth."

My heart was throbbing right along with the veins in my head. "Seriously? You're hardly older than me but she tells you everything, and I'm always left out." The words were spilling from my mouth, whiny and stupid as all heck, but I couldn't hold them in. "You love that, don't you? She can tell secrets to steady old Blake, but not to rage-monster Avery. I really hate you sometimes."

"Just get out, Avery. I can't deal with your tantrums."

I was *this* close to slamming the door and earning myself another week of dish duty, which would have been fabulous on top of all the extra garden work, but somehow I managed to take a breath and shut the door without breaking it off its hinges.

It was no use trying to get more information from Blake. Once he was riled up, his default setting was jerkface. But Mom was coming to the farm in a few days, and when she got here she was going to get a piece of my mind, for sure.

It sounded good in theory, anyway.

CHAPTER 12

I pretty much had to drag myself to Hollyhock Cottage the next day, what with that stolen key weighing like an anchor in my pocket. In the past, Grandma had always found me out, whether it was something simple like sneaking a cookie before lunch, or something twisted like slipping into Hilliard House and falling asleep for hours. What made me think I was safe now? Sure, it was hard to say no when Julian glowed with inspiration and treated me like a fellow filmmaker, but right then I was feeling a powerful urge to put the key back and call the whole thing off.

All that worrying pretty much fell out of my head when I knocked on the door of Hollyhock Cottage and it opened to a pretty girl who was several years younger than me. Her smile lit up her whole face.

"Are you Avery?" she asked.

"Yeah. Who are you?"

"I'm Lily. Didn't Julian tell you he had a sister?"

I stared like an idiot. She had long, dark hair that spilled over her shoulders in shiny ringlets. Her skin was several shades darker than Julian's.

"You don't look like him."

The dazzling smile vanished. "Julian told me you weren't a hick like everyone else around here."

Heat flushed my face. "Oh God, are you, like, adopted?"

Her mouth fell open. "Excuse me?"

I was starting to feel like the eight-year-old in this conversation, and the wheels in my brain were spinning like a truck in mud. I blinked, hoping I was hallucinating after all the hard work in the garden that morning, but she still stood there with her arms crossed, looking nothing like Julian.

Except for those eyes.

Julian and his dad had green eyes. So did Lily, but hers seemed huge in her little-girl face and were framed by long, thick lashes. She would be drop-dead gorgeous one day, and she was already better dressed than any girl I'd ever known. Her T-shirt and shorts looked about as expensive as Curtis Wayne's designer jeans, and even her flip-flops had fake diamonds on them. At least, I hoped they were fake.

"Right, I'm sorry. You're just so much . . . *prettier* than Julian."

She smiled at that. "Of course I am. Girls are pretty, and boys are handsome, and Dad says Julian will get better looking when he's older, but don't tell him I said that." Lily did a little bounce and wiggle, almost as if she had to pee. "Are you coming inside or what?"

"Oh, yeah, that'd be great." I could just see Grandma frowning at my manners. "It's very nice to meet you, Lily."

"Nice to meet you, too. I got here last night." She lowered her voice. "Julian told me about the *project*. I'm supposed to take you upstairs before—"

"Lily, is that Avery May at the door?" a voice called from within.

Lily's shoulders sank. "Yes, Daddy!"

"Bring her to the kitchen."

She mouthed "sorry" before turning to lead the way.

Curtis Wayne stood at the stove by a shiny kettle that sounded like it was about to boil. "Hey, Avery May. How about a cup of tea before you guys set out?"

As nice as it sounded to sit with Mr. Wayne sipping tea, it was hot as heck outside. "No thank you, sir."

He smiled and turned to Lily. "Go grab your hat, honey, and put sunscreen on your face. Your mother will kill me if you go back to Nashville with a peeling nose."

Lily scrunched up that pretty nose but didn't complain as she skipped out of the room.

The kettle started boiling for real then, and he quickly lifted it off the burner. "It always spooks me when it whistles."

I nodded, watching as he held the tag of the tea bag with one hand and poured with the other. He wore a T-shirt, which meant I could see the tattoo on his right arm—an intertwining design like you'd see in the borders of a medieval manuscript. He wasn't a beefy sort of guy, but he had nice muscles in his arms. And he always moved in a slow and steady way that told me he was comfortable in his own skin. I liked being near him.

"I'm going to have a cookie with my tea. Can I offer you a snickerdoodle?"

I was a little too nervous about Hilliard House to be hungry, but he seemed so eager to give me *something*. "Yes, please."

He grinned. "We can have a little sit-down while you wait for Julian."

I tried not to stare while I nibbled on the cookie, but part of me was comparing his face to that of the man in the photo with Mom. Another part of me imagined Mom meeting Curtis Wayne long ago and having children with him before he got to be a famous musician. Then I'd have a brother more like Julian. But even better, I'd have a dad, and it didn't even matter that he was rich and famous. I didn't care about his money, and that kind of made me proud of myself.

I jumped a little when he spoke.

"You sure look thoughtful, Avery May."

"Your daughter is nice." I rubbed a crumb from my chin. "But I made an idiot of myself when she opened the door. I thought she'd look more like Julian."

"Ah." He smiled. "She takes after her mother."

"But . . ."

"Julian's mother and I are divorced. Lily's mom is my second wife."

"Wow." I'd spent all this time with Julian, but I'd never asked much about his family. Then again, he seemed to shy away from talking about his dad. "Is it hard? I mean, is Julian mad at your wife for taking you away from his mom? Does he hold it against you?"

Mr. Wayne winced.

"That's what happened with a friend of mine back home," I said quickly, my cheeks crawling with heat. "I shouldn't be so nosy."

"It's okay. The whole world seems way too nosy about

my life, but I know you're not snooping for the tabloids." He glanced at me over the rim of his cup. "You're not hiding a microphone under that ponytail, are you?"

I gasped. "No way!"

Then I saw the twinkle in his eye.

"There's no 'stepmonster' business going on with us," he said. "She and Julian get along pretty well."

"What about his mom?"

He frowned. "I got custody, and Julian's lived with me since the divorce."

"Does he ever see her?"

Mr. Wayne leaned forward. "Are you sure you're not working for the tabloids?"

I giggled. "If I am, no one told me."

His eyes twinkled again, but with a blink they turned serious. "Julian's mom is very ill. She has been for a long time."

I started to ask what kind of illness, but something in his expression warned me off. "Julian seems okay, though. And Lily is cool."

"Yes, she is." His shoulders softened.

"And beautiful."

He smiled. "She wants to be an actress, and she's already getting small parts in commercials and music videos."

"I'm a swimmer, too." Lily appeared at the door, spreading a blob of sunscreen across her nose and cheeks. "Did Daddy tell you I was born in the water?"

"Literally," he said.

"I just came from swim camp. Swimming is my second-favorite thing. Want to hear my life plan?"

"Uh, sure," I said.

"First I train for the Olympics. After I win a few medals, I'll do sponsorships. *Then* I'll start acting full-time in movies."

Her face was perfectly straight as she told me this. And the crazy thing was, I didn't doubt she could tackle it all. For an eight-year-old she was pretty intense, but not in a bad way. Some people—like her and Julian—just knew what they wanted. Other people tended to wander between this and that, not really trying hard at anything. Like me.

Julian appeared behind Lily and pulled his backpack over both shoulders. He was wearing another funky T-shirt with a cartoon of some guy's head. Only this head was a simple outline that was shaped almost like a balloon. Or half of one, at least. Where did he get these shirts?

"Are we ready?" Julian asked. "If we don't leave now, Dad will make us have a tea party."

Lily giggled.

Mr. Wayne leaned forward and lightly tapped the cartoon on Julian's T-shirt. "By all means go make your movie, young Mr. Hitchcock. Just know that I'm counting on you to pay the bills when my career bottoms out, which it will if I don't get enough songs written this summer."

"Embrace your despair, Dad. It can be a great motivator."

Mr. Wayne waved us off with a laugh, but I saw something else in his eyes as I turned to follow Julian out the door. It looked a lot like worry.

CHAPTER 13

The sun was scorching, and by the time Hilliard House was in view I'd worked up a good sweat to go along with the dread boiling in my belly. Julian wiped his face on the sleeve of his shirt while Lily stared at the back of the house.

"It's so old," she said.

Julian and I followed as she walked around to get the front view. We all stood in silence while she took in the two stories of red brick and the fancy porch with its four white pillars and triangle-shaped roof. The paint was peeling from the trim and a few of the windows were cracked, but the brick was holding steady. Someone had whacked the weeds since Julian and I had been there last.

"It's a lot prettier from the front." Lily turned to Julian. "But there's no light in the window like in the photograph."

"If there was a light in the window," I said, "I'd be halfway back to Grandma's house by now."

"Really?" Julian studied me. "It bothers you that much?"

I shrugged. "Kind of."

"Well, you wouldn't see the light in the daytime anyway." Julian turned to Lily. "And we didn't come all the way out here just to get spooked and run away."

Lily put her hands on her hips. "But I *like* being spooked."

"I don't," I said.

In fact, butterflies flapped in my stomach as I put the key in the lock. It didn't turn at first, and for a second I was sure it would break off in the lock. The thought of having to explain that to Grandma was almost scarier than the prospect of a ghost on the other side of the door.

"This place is starting to seem a little creepy now," whispered Lily.

"Try pushing on the door as you turn the key," Julian said.

When I did that, the dead bolt released. My shoulders tensed up as I opened the door, but the only thing to fly out at me was a rush of stale-smelling air.

The door creaked as it swung wide to reveal a hallway and staircase. On either side, a double door opened to a large room. Above us dangled a dusty old light fixture with fake candles. By the looks of the furniture left behind, the room at our right had been a dining room. The room at our left had a large fireplace, so it must have been a parlor.

That meant it was the parlor window Julian had pointed out in his photo—the one that clearly showed a light shining in it. A light in a house that hadn't been occupied for years.

"It smells like old people in here," said Lily. "And death."

"Lily, you have no idea what death smells like." Julian shook his head as he unzipped his backpack.

"I'm pretty sure it smells like this," she muttered.

The place did have a strong smell—mildew, old newspapers, and rusty pipes came to mind. Definitely a whiff of mouse droppings, but even Grandma found mice in her house sometimes, so that didn't bother me. She always said you couldn't blame the creatures for trying to find shelter, and if they were faster than Weasley, more power to them.

"Does it look the same to you, Avery?"

I jumped a little at Julian's voice. "I was younger than Lily back then, and I barely remember anything except Grandma walloping my backside." I turned to find him checking his camera. "So what's the plan? Are you taking photos today?"

Julian strapped the camera around his neck and set the backpack by the door. "I thought I might start filming."

"Filming what? We haven't even started the script."

And I'd really been looking forward to writing that script because it would finally get us to *my* specialty.

He stared past me, his brow wrinkling. "I want to improvise as much as possible. The film will look more natural that way. Today I'll just film you and Lily exploring the house."

"I thought that camera was for taking pictures."

"Did you think I'd be rolling in a full-size camera on a dolly or something? This camera also shoots HD video. And it's all we've got."

I held up my hands. "Fine."

He attached a long, foam-covered object to the top of the camera. "On a real set you have a boom operator who holds this big fuzzy microphone on a long stick. His job is to get close enough to pick up the sound while still keeping the boom out of the frame." He nodded at the foam microphone. "This is the best I can do with what we have."

"Your camera has a horn!" said Lily, grinning.

"Anyway . . ." Julian gave her a sidelong glance. "Let's go back outside so I can film you two unlocking the door. We might use it later, or we might not, but best to get it done now. Just remember to act like you're doing it for the first time."

After we took care of that, Julian told me to lead the way through the dining room. The windows had those old-fashioned paper shades rolled halfway down. Both were torn and crooked, and the windowsills were full of fly corpses. I turned back to the large table, running my hand across its surface to trace the scars and burns. A battered hutch stood against the wall, but it held no plates or glassware.

The mildew and mouse smells were stronger in the kitchen, and some of the cabinet doors hung off their hinges. There was a fridge, but it looked about a hundred years old. I bet Joshua Hilliard spent as little time as possible in the kitchen after his wife died. Probably ate out of cans or made cold-cut sandwiches. The room seemed lonely, as if it didn't know what to do with itself.

"Ewww." Lily pointed at the floor. "There's a dried-up mouse over here. Get a shot of this, Jules."

I glanced at Julian. "What does a dead mouse have to do with anything?"

"No, she's right," he said. "Look how it's mummified."

He took about twenty close-ups of the mummy mouse. When he turned back around, I raised an eyebrow at him, but he just shrugged.

After that we passed by an empty room and a sad little powder room—more mildew stink and rust stains in the sink—and then made our way back to the parlor.

This room was different. I could feel something shift inside me when we walked through the wide doorway. Maybe it was the huge brick fireplace or the yellowed curtains that still had some prettiness to them, but this room lifted my spirits. Like it was haunted by the ghost of happiness.

Which made no sense at all. Why would a happy person stick around after death?

I went to the fireplace and touched the wood mantel. Dusty cobwebs stretched beneath it, but above it was a framed photograph of an old house with white wood siding and a two-level porch that stretched all the way across. I'd seen a small version of this photo in Grandpa's album.

"This was the first house on the farm," I said to Lily. "The one that burned down."

"Did anyone die in the fire?"

"Grandma didn't know."

Lily frowned. "There could be ghosts here from the old house." She walked to the window opposite the fireplace. "Was this where the light was shining?"

Julian was still filming, so I answered Lily with a nod. We all stood quiet for a moment, and a nervous twinge started up in my belly. The two of them seemed to be waiting for something exciting to happen, as if the old kerosene lamp on the table would suddenly light itself. A part of me *wanted* that to happen because Julian would be impressed.

Another part of me knew I would pee my pants if that lamp decided to light itself right before our eyes.

Lily yawned. "This room is boring. Let's go upstairs."

Julian let the camera run a moment longer and then lowered it. "I want to film you two walking up the staircase, but first let me make sure the stairs are safe."

After testing the steps, he made us walk up the staircase slowly, saying it'd be more dramatic that way. I swear the temperature rose a couple degrees with each step, and by the time we got to the top I felt a little dizzy and a lot sweaty. There were two doors at our left and three at the right. The nearest door opened to a small bathroom with a pedestal sink, a toilet, and a dirty tub.

Lily turned the knob at the sink. After some creepy glugging noises, a glop of brown water spurted out. We both jumped at that. After more sputtering, the water flowed stronger and mostly clear.

Julian lowered his camera. "You'd think the water would be turned off since no one lives here."

"Grandma must have told the water company to turn it on since she's selling the house," I said. "We may not have much time to film. She already got someone to trim the weeds outside, so she'll probably be sending someone here to clean any day now."

Julian fiddled with the tub faucet. Again, there was a spell of glugging before the water spurted out.

"Interesting," he said. "Once your grandma gets in here and cleans up, the house won't look right for the film. We really can't waste any time."

Taking this to heart, Lily marched toward the first bedroom on our right, and I followed her lead. This bedroom, and the next, and the one after that, had peeling floral wallpaper and dusty braided rugs on the floor. Each contained some part of a bed—a headboard or frame—but no mattresses. In one room, the old bed frame stood near a fireplace and was draped with a quilt. The binding was frayed and torn, and the quilt needed a good washing, but it was still pretty. Lily shook her head at the old bed and marched right out of the room, but Julian stayed in the doorway filming.

I leaned over the quilt to get a closer look. The quilter had stitched initials in a corner block—s.f.—but I couldn't match those letters to anyone in our family. The entire thing was handmade, just like the ones at Grandma's house, and probably made from the scraps of old clothes. The one on my bed in Grandma's attic still had all its stitches and was softer than any blanket you'd ever find in a store. I patted this quilt like it was kinfolk and wondered why it was here instead of in some cousin's home.

"Hey, come in here!" Lily shouted from the other side of the house.

Julian was still filming, and he gestured for me to go around him.

I found Lily in the small corner bedroom, which was papered with a delicate pattern of rosebuds. A twin bed frame stood in the corner next to a chest of drawers.

"This was propped up against the bed." Lily held out a doll in a pink dress. "Watch the head. It's coming loose."

I took the doll, cradling her head carefully. She was made of china, with molded golden waves for hair. Her small eyes and mouth were painted on, along with large pink circles on the cheeks. Her arms and legs were china, too, and plain brown boots were painted on her tiny little feet. The pink dress was dusty and faded but not stained, though it did smell mousy.

"Isn't she creepy?" Lily's eyes glowed with excitement.

"Not really. Maybe if she had eyes that opened and closed, or if she spoke—"

"Look under the dress," Lily interrupted.

I slowly lifted the skirt, only to find a yellowed petticoat and bloomers underneath.

"Lift it higher," she urged, "but don't drop her, Avery!"

The torso of the doll was cloth filled with stuffing. Or at least it had been once. Something had torn the belly open and pulled the stuffing out. The cavity was dotted with mouse droppings.

"It's like a doll murderer ripped her guts out," Lily stage-whispered.

I'm not really the squeamish type, but for some reason I had to turn my head away from the doll to take a breath. "You watch too much late-night TV," I finally said. "A mama mouse made a home in her belly, is all. Maybe some baby mice were born here, all warm and cozy."

"Ugh! Remind me to wash my hands." She took the doll and set it on the chest of drawers. "I also found this in the bottom drawer." She pulled a small frame of tarnished silver from her pocket and handed it to me.

The photo was a faded black-and-white shot of two girls squinting as if they faced the sun. One was small with straight dark hair and a body that was pointy all over—sharp chin, knees, and elbows. The other girl had a little more flesh to squeeze, and I pointed at her dandelion hair, round and light gold, just like the china doll's hair.

"That's Margaret Anne," I whispered.

"I know," Lily said quietly.

I glanced at her. "How?"

"This was *her* room, and that was her doll," said Lily. "I can feel her here."

I looked around me. "I don't feel anything."

Only that was a lie, because goose bumps were crawling up my arms.

Julian stepped through the doorway to film Lily as she walked around the room. Her fingers trailed along the wallpaper and plucked at the yellowed curtains.

When she'd walked the entire room, Lily turned to face me. "I think she likes me."

"What?"

"She wants me to be her friend. I'm close to her age, after all." Her mouth curved in a coy smile. Julian kept filming, even though Lily was now still and silent. I squirmed as a blob of sweat traveled down my spine.

A creaking broke the silence. I turned to see the bedroom door slowly swinging toward the doorframe.

All on its own.

A strange pressure filled my ears, almost like when an airplane starts its descent before landing. Time seemed to slow down as I watched that door inching along. When it shut, it *slammed,* and my ears popped so hard I nearly bit my tongue.

"What the heck?" I blurted.

We'd each frozen in place, not one of us within arm's length of the door, and my heart was thumping like crazy.

Julian moved first, lowering his camera and reaching for the doorknob. Taking a breath, he opened it and peered outside.

"There's no one there," he said.

I craned my neck to see beyond him to the hallway. "Did either of you hear footsteps?"

"I didn't," said Lily. "The door slammed all by itself."

"But something happened to my ears," I said. "What was that?"

Julian took his hand off the knob, and the door swung closed again, very slowly and this time without latching. "It was probably a draft," he said. "The floors might be uneven—that's pretty common in old houses."

"Or maybe Margaret Anne slammed the door," said Lily.

"Oh, come on!" I said. "Why would she do that?"

Lily's eyes widened. "Maybe she's trying to tell us something."

CHAPTER 14

On our way back to Hollyhock Cottage, Lily skipped ahead as if nothing weird had happened. Julian walked beside me without saying a word. I knew he was thinking hard, though, because he was frowning.

"What happened back there?" I finally asked. "Was Lily just playing?"

He shrugged. "The door is easy to explain. It's hard to say about Lily. She's pretty sensitive."

"What does that mean?"

"She picks up on things others don't." He turned to me. "Do you believe in ghosts?"

A fresh crop of goose bumps sprang up on my arms. "Before this summer, I just tried not to think about them. The *idea* of ghosts scares me a lot, though."

He nodded as if he understood.

I took a breath. "You know how I told you about sneaking into Hilliard House?"

"Yeah, and your grandma took a belt to you, right? Which seems totally over the top, but whatever."

"Well, I didn't tell you the whole story."

Julian raised an eyebrow but didn't say anything.

"I actually fell asleep in the house, and Grandma ended up calling the sheriff. There was even a search party."

"Wow. What did you say when they found you?"

"I don't know. All I remember are flashing lights and Grandma's face. She was full of *wrath*, Julian. I mean, Grandma can be strict and kinda preachy, but inside she's got a soft heart." I looked him straight in the eye. "That night when we got home? She became a different person with that belt. She'd never hurt me before. Come to think of it, she never has since."

He was quiet for a moment. "Well, you're a little too old for a spanking, if that's what you're afraid of."

"There's more—something my brother told me just a few days ago. I used to go to the house a lot. I don't remember it, but Blake said he followed me once. And when he was standing on the porch he heard me talking to someone inside. But no one else was there."

Julian's eyes brightened. "You mean you talked to a ghost? Was it Margaret Anne?"

"It could have been."

He looked thoughtful. "Maybe it's a good thing for you to go back to the house. My therapist would say it's therapeutic."

I blinked. "You have a therapist?"

"Yeah. So do half the kids at my school. Anyway, you'll be able to meet us at the house again tomorrow, right?"

"Sure." I paused. "No, wait. Tomorrow is Saturday. Mom's flying in from Dallas to spend a few days."

Julian sighed. "Well . . . that's okay, really. Lily and I

can get some footage on our own. You just have to loan me the key."

I stopped in my tracks. "You'd film *without* me?"

"We're running out of time. Tomorrow and Sunday Lily and I can get some of the boring stuff out of the way—you know, establishing shots and other stuff like that. The three of us can finish up on Monday or Tuesday. And I think we'll have enough footage for a cool short film. I never meant it to be longer than ten or fifteen minutes."

The thought of being left out of two days of filming—even two *hours* of filming—made my stomach feel hollow and achy. "So . . . what exactly is the story? Two girls wandering around a house?"

"Don't worry, Avery. You and I will find the story when we edit the footage. Right now all I need is the key."

I was extra glad to have Weasley in bed with me that night. He was pretty chilled out for a cat, and his rumbling purr always settled me down when I was agitated. But even with him curled up against my belly, my brain still raced.

Lily's whole act about "sensing" Margaret Anne had given me the heebie-jeebies while we were at the house, but over dinner I'd shrugged it off as a little kid's overactive imagination. That was a lot harder to do in the near dark of the attic. I replayed that slamming door over and over in my head, wondering what Margaret Anne might be trying to tell us. Was she warning us off? Or telling us to pay closer attention?

After Weasley moved to the foot of the bed, I tossed and

wriggled until I fell into another strange dream about Hilliard House. This time I was inside the house . . . in the parlor, actually, sitting on the rug and looking up at the mantel. That old china doll sat there, staring straight ahead. When my eyes moved to the framed photograph, something flickered on the glass—a reflection of movement. I heard a scratching sound behind me, but I couldn't seem to turn. I couldn't move at all.

I woke to the sound of Weasley scratching at the door to get out, and that meant turning on the lamp and stumbling down the stairs—*quietly*—to let him out of the attic. When I got back to the bed, I pulled the Kingdom box out, hoping to chase that spooky dream from my mind.

But the instant I lifted the lid, I knew it wouldn't work. The pages were limp and musty. Lifeless. The Kingdom magic had pretty much disappeared.

Crouching there in the near dark, I knew it had been slipping away for a while now. It was kind of like Christmas, when your heart yearned for a time when you really felt the magic. You hadn't looked for it, it just *was*. And forever after you were trying to find it again, to relive something you stumbled into and didn't appreciate while it lasted.

I shoved the box under the bed again and tried to go back to sleep. Which meant I spent another eternity tossing and turning while the air conditioner's creepy shudders and wheezes got louder with each minute. Finally I turned on the lamp and checked the clock. It felt like I'd been thrashing around in that bed for twenty hours at least, but it was only a little after midnight.

And that's when my bladder decided I really needed to pee.

I stepped into my slippers and crept down the stairs as softly as possible, somehow managing to avoid all the creaky floorboards on my way to the bathroom. I even got myself on the toilet without turning the light on.

But for some reason I couldn't stop my stupid hand from pressing the stupid handle to flush. It totally blew my stealth mode. By the time I'd washed and dried my hands and opened the door, Grandma was standing there in her flowery nightgown and robe.

"Are you sick, Avery May?"

"No, ma'am. I just had to pee."

Grandma looked more concerned than mad, but my throat started to ache and my eyes were prickling like I was going to cry or something.

"You want to come sit with me in the living room for a bit?" she asked.

Once we were settled on the sagging couch with my head nestled in the crook of her arm, that sudden urge to cry dried up. Grandma smelled comfortable—like soap and Jergen's lotion—and though the skin on her arms was loose and crinkly, her muscles were still strong as she held me tight.

"I couldn't sleep," I finally said.

She gave me a squeeze. "Something on your mind?"

I pondered how to explain it all . . . without *really* explaining it.

"You know how Julian and I are making a movie? About the history of the farm?"

Grandma nodded slowly. "Is that not going well?"

"It's going okay. But when Julian and I were in the cemetery, we saw the gravestone for Joshua Hilliard's wife and daughter. I saw . . . I mean, I couldn't help noticing that his daughter died when she was young. *Really* young."

She pulled me closer. "Have you been fixating on death, Avery May? Is that what has you so troubled?"

I squirmed. "Sort of. Julian said that the girl, Margaret Anne, died the same year as the floods in this area. He thinks she drowned, and I was just wondering if that was true."

"To be honest, I don't know. All your grandpa ever said was that it was Joshua Hilliard's fault. Samuel didn't care for the man, even though he was close kin."

"Why? What'd Joshua do?"

"For one thing, he left the church pretty early on in his life. Must have been after the war."

A twisty feeling came to my gut. Leaving the church was just about the worst thing a Hilliard could do. I should know, because Mom did it and Grandma still hadn't forgiven her.

"I never knew the wife or the daughter, but I do know that Joshua Hilliard turned peculiar in his old age. Hardly ever left the house, never wanted anyone to visit him." She shook her head. "Well, your mother sometimes took it into her head to walk out to that house and talk to him—"

"*Mom* was there?"

"Oh, I put a stop to that. It wasn't safe. And after he died, when I went into that house to see about getting it cleaned up? Well, I hardly know how to describe it. Avery May, there was a strangeness to that place."

I sat up. "You mean, like a ghost?"

"I was taught not to believe in that sort of nonsense. And yet, it was as if the house had held in bad thoughts and feelings for too long, and they'd festered terribly—and when

I opened that door they all rushed over me." She snorted. "That day I told myself I'd never go back in Hilliard House. It could fall into a pile of rubble for all I cared. And I didn't go back, at least not until . . ."

"Not until I fell asleep there."

"And nearly scared the wits right out of my head. I can't imagine what drew you to that house in the first place."

"I don't remember, Grandma."

"You're better off for it, I say." She gave me a quick squeeze and then looked me straight in the eye. "You stay away from that house, Avery May. It's a place of darkness."

CHAPTER 15

Saturday's drive to Nashville was miserable as usual. Grandma's car was small and basic, but it *did* have air-conditioning. She just didn't like the air blowing in her face, so she set it to the lowest level and vented the air to the floorboard. It wasn't so bad for those sitting up front, but as the youngest and smallest, I was always stuck in the back. And because Grandma drove at least a hundred miles under the speed limit, it took us two stuffy, sweaty hours to get to the airport.

That drive gave me a lot of time to think about Mom. I always missed her during our summers in Tennessee. Don't get me wrong—it was great to have a break from the school-year schedule. I loved running free on the farm with Blake, and most of all I'd looked forward to getting back to Kingdom. But it only took a week for me to miss Mom's cooking. To miss the cool of her hand stroking my cheek. I always stood as close as possible to the airport security exit so I'd be the first one she saw when she came through, and her face always broke into a wide smile at the sight of me. It even gave me a warm feeling in my belly to see her hug Blake. Any other time he would cringe at her attempts to squeeze him—like he might be contaminated by Mom cooties, or something—but he never shied away from that airport hug.

I still looked forward to seeing Mom, of course, but now the mystery man in the photo hovered between us. She hadn't lied to my face about him, but she'd kept the truth from me. Grandma would have called that a "lie of omission."

Who was he, and how had she met him? What had she loved about him? Why couldn't she just be a regular mom and have babies before she divorced him? A lot of people I knew, including Julian, had parents who weren't actually married to each other anymore. But they still had both parents. At the very least, they knew the names of both parents.

I would never know my father's name.

It had bothered me for a long time—ever since I started school—but this summer had stirred up a real anger about it. I had no idea how to explain this to Mom, though. Maybe that was why I was a little stiff when she came through the security exit. I felt torn down the middle—half my heart leaping at first sight of her while the other half seethed over her secrets and lies.

"Avery, it's so good to see you!" She crushed me in a bear hug. When she pulled back, her forehead creased. "There's something different about you, sweetie."

"Yeah?"

"It's only been a week, but you look *older*. How can that be?" She shook her head. "Why can't you stay my baby forever?"

I couldn't help grinning at that. Actually, it was nice to have everyone smiling, even Blake. I had plenty of time to ask her about the husband thing. It could wait until Monday at least. A day and a half of peace wouldn't hurt anybody.

"I want to know what's been going on," Mom said at the supper table after the blessing. "I mean, since you two are taking a break from Kingdom this summer."

I turned to Blake—he was the one responsible for the break, after all—but he just shoveled a pile of mashed potatoes into his mouth and stared back at me. Fortunately Grandma jumped in.

"Blake's been working on his summer-reading list." She patted my hand. "And Avery May has a new friend. She's been spending a lot of time with him."

"*Him?*" Mom's head snapped up. "Avery, did you tell me about this?"

"It's not like that, Maddie," said Grandma. "I've met the boy—he's spending the summer with his father at Hollyhock Cottage."

Blake reached for the last drumstick. "His dad's a country music star."

"Oh, really?" Mom turned to look at me. "What's his name?"

"Curtis Wayne," I mumbled.

Her eyes widened. "Are you kidding me?"

I shook my head. "I didn't know he was famous until Julian explained."

"I've seen him in the commercials for those country music awards shows." Mom grinned. "What would you and your friends call him? A *hottie*?"

"God, Mom!"

"Avery, what have I said about taking the Lord's name in vain?" Grandma took a deep breath. "Mr. Wayne seems quite amiable. Not at all full of himself like you might expect from a celebrity. His daughter arrived a couple of days ago, and Avery May is working on a project with both children."

"A project? Tell me all about it, Avery."

I picked at the skin on my chicken breast. First of all, I *had* told Mom about the film. Second, I'd been so distracted by secret husbands and ghost girls that I'd forgotten to think of a good answer to the whole "what's it about" question.

"I told you on the phone, Mom," I stalled. "We're, um, making a movie together."

"I'm sorry, honey. I must have been really tired that night. Remind me what the movie is about."

"We're just filming scenes here and there on the farm. It's kind of a history of the place. Julian says it's going to be a 'short'—only about fifteen minutes long."

"She's totally into this movie, Mom," said Blake. "You wouldn't believe how seriously Avery's taking it." He looked directly at me. "She'll stop at *nothing*."

I shot back the dirtiest look I could manage. "It's not that big a deal."

"Hilliard Farm history, huh? Maybe Mama could put the video on her website." Mom glanced at Grandma. "That is, if she'd finally join the twenty-first century and make a website for her rental cottage."

"It's not worth the bother, Maddie. I gave the important details to that Tennessee rental cottage website, and if someone needs to know more, they call. Sometimes even that's more than I want to fool with."

"It would simplify things if you let people book online. All you need is satellite TV for an Internet connection." When Grandma only grunted in response, Mom turned back to me. "I look forward to seeing your movie, Avery."

Thank goodness she switched focus to Blake at that point, because I was not cool with talking about the movie. Mom could *never* see it. If she did, she'd know I broke Grandma's rules. That I stole the key and snuck into an abandoned house. And then she'd probably find out about me falling asleep in Hilliard House all those years ago, because she's a lawyer and she's good at getting facts out of people who don't want to share them. And that would cause another huge argument between her and Grandma. And maybe she'd never let me come to Tennessee again.

Mom set down her napkin and smiled at Grandma. "That was delicious, Mama. I'm trying to cut back on meat, but you know I never can resist your fried chicken." She turned to Blake. "If you'll clear the table, I'll wash the dishes. Avery, would you mind helping me with the drying?"

This was the point when Grandma would herd Blake off to the living room so that I could have Mom all to myself. And there was so much I wanted to ask her. Like, who exactly was this man she'd married and why hadn't I ever heard of him? I also wanted to know more about Joshua Hilliard, seeing as she'd known him.

But I'd told myself to wait until later to deal with all that, so I just stood there fiddling with the towel while she filled the sink with soapy water.

"What's on your mind, Avery?"

After a bit more fiddling, I decided it was easier to talk about myself for now. "It's this movie I'm making with Julian. He and his sister did some filming without me today, and it made me feel kind of . . ."

"Left out?"

"Yeah. And I won't see them again until Monday." I took a glass from her to dry. "I mean, I'll see them on Monday if it's okay with you. We usually just work for a couple of hours or so."

She eyed me for a moment. "This project is pretty important to you, isn't it?"

I nodded.

"Then I want you to finish it." She smiled. "Thanks for considering my feelings. That's awfully grown-up of you."

I couldn't meet her eyes for long, so I walked the dried glass over to the cabinet. "Julian and I have been doing research for the film, and we learned about Joshua Hilliard. Grandma says you talked to him sometimes, and that she didn't like it."

Mom paused in her washing. "Wow, I haven't thought about Mr. Hilliard in a long while."

"Was he scary? Old men scare me sometimes."

She ran water over a plate and handed it to me. "I know what you mean, but no. Mostly he was just sad. He'd lived alone in that house for such a long time."

"Grandma said he was dark and *maudlin*."

"'Maudlin' is a good word—remember it for the SATs. But it's not really how I remember him. Mr. Hilliard was very kind. Gentlemanly, even. Mama didn't like me going in the house, but sometimes he'd be working outside, or sitting on his front step, and he'd offer me a butterscotch candy."

"Mom! Candy from a stranger?"

"He was family, Avery. And he always seemed pleased to see me." She paused. "You know, he talked to me like I mattered. Like he cared about my opinions. But after a while he'd get a faraway look, and I knew he needed to be alone again. Figured he was missing his family."

"So why is he buried separately from them?"

Mom shook her head sadly. "That's how his wife wanted it."

"Isn't that kind of strange?"

"I knew better than to pry."

I took a breath. "Did he tell you about his daughter? The one who died so young?"

She glanced sidelong at me as she handed over the chicken platter. "Well, aren't you the little investigative reporter!"

"You've never told us much about our family history," I said.

She studied me for a moment before plunging her hands back in the water. "Mr. Hilliard didn't talk about his daughter much. I expect it was too painful, and I can understand that. If I lost you or Blake . . . Well, I can't even bear to imagine what I'd do." She shook her head and pulled the sink plug. "Speaking of Blake, he seems a little subdued."

"Yeah, I know. He's totally wrapped up in his own stupid stuff."

Mom tilted her head as if to study me. "Actually, I'd say he seems a little lonely."

"I seriously doubt that."

"But you've been spending all your time with the boy down the road. And you're working on a pretty complicated project together. Did you ever think of inviting Blake to join in?"

I stared at her. "Mom, I already told you. *He blew me off.* He doesn't want to do Kingdom anymore. He acts like it's just baby stuff." I took a breath. "Maybe it *is* a kid thing, but he didn't have to be so rude about it."

"Tell me what he said exactly."

"He said he was starting high school in the fall and was done playing magical kingdoms, or whatever." Coming out of my mouth, the words had about as much impact as a foam football. "I don't know . . . it just really hurt my feelings."

"Did you even try to talk to him about it? To think of other things to do together?"

"Um . . . no. I pretty much just screamed at him."

She raised an eyebrow.

"Yeah, yeah, I get it, Mom. I have anger issues."

She put her damp hands on my cheeks and kissed my forehead. "Just think about what we've talked about. That's all I ask."

CHAPTER 16

When I knocked at the cottage door on Monday afternoon, Curtis Wayne opened it. "Lily hasn't slept too well the past couple of nights," he said in a low voice. "I told her she'd better take a nap before she went filming with you. Want to come sit with me and Julian until she wakes up?"

That was totally fine with me, but Julian didn't look pleased to be stuck at the kitchen table. Actually, it was more that he looked *jumpy.* His right foot tapped the floor, and his eyes didn't stay focused on one thing for more than a couple of seconds.

Curtis Wayne clapped his hands together, and it wasn't even that loud, but Julian jumped a little anyway. "Today's offering is a classic: Curtis Wayne's Extra-Fantastic Chocolate Chip Cookies. No messy chocolate chunks, no yucky nuts. Just the perfect combination of dough and chips. Delicious with milk." He turned to me. "How about it, Avery May? Are you up for cookies and milk?"

I hadn't eaten much at lunch, and my stomach had been rumbling since I walked through the door. "Yes, please, sir!"

"Julian?"

"I'm not hungry." His foot was still tapping away. "Should I go check if Lily's awake yet?"

"She'll come down when she's ready, just like always." Mr. Wayne studied Julian for a moment. "Can I talk with you in the living room, son?"

"You can say whatever you need to say right here."

My cheeks prickled with heat, and I could feel my body shrinking into itself.

Mr. Wayne took a breath. "All right. Have you taken your medication today?"

Julian stared back without flinching. "Yes."

"Really? Because you seem a little on edge."

Julian stilled his foot. "I'm just ready to get filming," he said slowly. "That's all."

"Really?"

"Yeah, Dad, that's all."

Mr. Wayne's face drooped, and my heart went out to him. While he poured the milk and set out the cookies, I did the only thing I could think of to fill the awkward silence.

I babbled.

I talked about Mom, and how she and Grandma weren't speaking because yesterday she'd made "a spectacle of herself"—Grandma's exact words—by refusing to take Communion. That put me on the topic of Grandma's church and the grape juice Communion, and how I thought everyone drank grape juice for Communion until I went to a Lutheran service with a friend of mine, and . . . Oh, it was pretty much what Blake would call "verbal diarrhea." Half the time I had no idea what would come out of my mouth next, but at least I was filling the air with something other than hurt.

I settled back in pure relief when Lily finally appeared in the doorway. She was dressed in shorts and a T-shirt with her hair pulled back in a sparkly hair tie and a bejeweled hat on her head. Her nose and cheeks were already coated with sunscreen, and she smelled like coconut.

Julian stood as soon as he saw her.

"Hold on, son." Mr. Wayne straightened in his chair. "Let Lily have a glass of milk at least."

Lily glanced from father to brother, her eyes wide. "I'm ready. I don't need anything."

Julian's shoulders slumped. "Have a cookie, Lil. It's okay."

I'd been holding my breath for what seemed like forever, and finally I let it go.

Only it came out as a belch.

Lily grinned. "Good one, Avery." She reached for the milk her dad had just poured. "But I can do better."

When we finally were on our way, Lily skipped ahead to chase a butterfly. Or maybe she was trying to escape the dark cloud around her brother. An hour ago I'd had a million things to say to Julian, but now I wasn't sure if he'd bite my head off or just ignore me. I couldn't be blamed for having heard he was on medication, could I?

After several more minutes of dead silence, I couldn't take it anymore.

"So . . . what's your deal?"

He was quiet for so long, I was sure he was mad at me. Just as I was opening my mouth to apologize, he finally spoke.

"Dad thinks I'm getting too obsessed with this project,

and that I'm wearing Lily out. I told him we're on the clock because your grandma's about to sell the place, but he keeps asking questions. I don't want to lie to him about being at Hilliard House without your grandma's permission."

"Or about making me steal the key."

He glanced at me. "I can't *make* you do anything, Avery. I just encouraged you to take a risk for the sake of art."

I pondered that for a moment. "Okay . . . What's with the medication?"

His jaw tightened. "It's no big deal. It just helps me focus."

"Then why were you so rude to your dad about it?"

He sighed. "He's always watching me like I'm a ticking time bomb. It's because of my mother, and it's really starting to get on my nerves."

"Your dad told me she was sick."

"He did?" Julian shook his head. "Wow, he usually doesn't talk about it with anyone outside of the family."

"Does she have cancer or something?"

"No. Schizophrenia."

I thought for a moment. "Does that mean she sees things that aren't there?"

"She's crazy, Avery." Julian swallowed hard. "I mean that literally. It's so bad that she has to stay at a care facility and take a lot of meds." His chin dropped. "I don't see her much anymore. I guess it upsets her too much."

I didn't know what to say, so I just watched him out of the corner of my eye.

"I don't remember how she was before she got sick," he continued. "I just wish Dad wasn't always so scared I'll go off the rails because of her. I mean, a lot of creative people are intense and anxious—it doesn't mean the doctor needs to up my dosage." He turned to me. "You're lucky your dad is dead and you never have to deal with the pushing and worrying. Or the disappearing act."

"I'd rather have a pushy, worried dad, even one that wasn't always around, than no dad at all."

"You wouldn't say that if you were in my position. What was your dad like before he died?"

I waited for the panic. The flush of shame mixed with anger. But it didn't come. I'd never felt so calm when faced with the dad question. I guess I'd never met anyone who actually needed to know the truth. But at the moment, Julian needed to know.

"My father isn't dead. Actually, he might be, but I'll never know."

"Why?" Julian lurched to a halt and turned to me. "Were you adopted?"

"My dad was a test tube," I said. "Some guy's . . . you know . . . was frozen and then put inside my mom. She says he was a med student who, um, made a donation for cash and the promise that he'd stay anonymous. I will *never* get to meet him. Or even if I did, I wouldn't know it was him."

Julian stared at me. And then he stared some more. I could almost hear the second hand of the earth's clock ticking as he continued to stare at me.

"Are you still going to be my friend, Julian?"

He flinched. "What does your dad being a sperm donor have to do with us being friends? Are you ashamed or something?"

"No!" I kicked at the ground. "Well, maybe a little. Sometimes I hate Mom for putting this on me. The sperm donor kid. Seems like someone asks me about my dad every day, and what can I say except that he's dead? That shuts people up. Telling the truth just would open up the biggest can of awkward."

I gave him a sidelong glance. He didn't look too sympathetic.

"Blake's not bothered by the whole deal," I said. "He tells people he doesn't have a dad, which pretty much is true, and people don't bug him about it. But with me it's different. I have to lie."

"Why?"

"I just do." Tears pricked my eyes. "It's not fair. I never had a choice."

"No one has a choice about who their parents are."

"But most people get a chance to *know* their parents, and my mom took that chance away from me."

Julian wiped his forehead on his sleeve. "Avery, I can't really know how you feel, but . . . I'm sorry this dad thing upsets you."

I swallowed. "Thanks . . . I guess?"

"Are you okay now?"

"Not really, but that won't keep me from filming."

"Good." He looked at the ground. "Because I was thinking . . . maybe you should get behind the camera today."

"What?"

"You can film the scenes."

Me? With the camera? A mix of joy and fear swirled in my stomach, and the whole dad conversation might as well have happened a million years ago. This was getting real.

This was getting . . . *awesome.*

CHAPTER 17

Of course Julian took about a century getting the camera set for filming. Lily lost patience and wandered up the staircase. I tried to follow what he was doing, but the thing might as well have been alien technology. He stared at the LCD screen and pushed buttons like it was a video game controller, and the camera beeped and clicked as if they were having a conversation.

"I'll explain this to you sometime," he said. "For now we just need to get going. When we're back at the cottage, I'll show you the footage Lily and I took on Saturday. I've already edited some of it."

"You *edited* without me, too?"

"Just a little. We didn't even film that much, and I'll show you exactly what I did. It's pretty cool." He snapped the microphone into place and plugged its skinny cord into the side of the camera. Then he held the camera away from him, framing the staircase in the LCD screen. After pushing a few more buttons, he glanced at me. "Are you ready?"

He put the strap around my neck and placed the camera in my hands. It was heavier than I'd expected. I put my hands around it just as he had, my index finger finding the On/Off button and the shutter release. Julian showed me how to activate the video function with my thumb, and then he made me practice taking a little footage.

"Hold it steady, but don't worry if it shakes a little," he said. "Shaky cam is popular now. It adds a cool level of immediacy."

"What's that mean?"

"It's when viewers feel like they're in the moment. Part of the action. It makes things seem more exciting."

I glanced around the foyer, considering the options. "Where should we start?"

Lily appeared at the top of the staircase. "I think y'all should come up here."

Julian nodded. "Come back down first so we can film you walking up the stairs. Avery, don't worry if you mess up. We can edit later."

I tried to make my steps smooth and steady as I followed Lily up the stairs, but there definitely were some shaky cam moments. Lily did a good job of being dramatic as she climbed each step, her hand sliding along the banister. I mean, it wasn't overdone or anything. Somehow she used the set of her shoulders and the trembling in her hand to show excitement *and* nervousness to the camera. At one point she glanced back, her eyes wide and her hair a little wild. It was perfect.

But a funny feeling swirled in my stomach when she headed directly to Margaret Anne's room. I guess we really didn't *know* it belonged to the poor little girl. Lily was certain, though, and something about that bothered me. Or maybe it was the room that bothered me.

Lily went straight for the chest of drawers. She smoothed the dress on the china doll and touched her finger to its lips like a kiss. Then she picked up the photo of Margaret Anne, stroking the frame with her thumbs. She actually knelt on the floor with that photo, almost like she was praying to it. I glanced back at Julian, but he just made that winding gesture with his hands that meant *keep filming.* So I did, even though the funny feeling in my stomach was churning faster and my hands were starting to ache from filming such a long take.

"Margaret Anne . . . I'm here," said Lily softly. Her body rocked back and forth, and I nailed the shaky cam technique without even trying.

"Margaret Anne?" Lily tilted her head as if she was listening. "I hear you now. I feel you near me." Her little body shivered as if a chill had come to the air. But it was hot and sticky on that second floor.

"You seem so sad," Lily said. "Why do you stay here in this house? Why can't you be free?"

I glanced at Julian again. A dizziness crept over me—warm and prickly—and my hands were so sweaty I was afraid I'd drop the camera.

He nodded encouragingly.

I turned back to Lily, who clutched that little photo to her chest and kept on rocking. Her eyes were shut tight. In fact, she'd scrunched up her face as if she was in pain.

"Margaret Anne, I see it now," she breathed. "I see what you saw. I'm at the edge of the water, and I just want to dip my feet. The water's never been this high before. I've never been able to step right into it. It feels so cold rushing over my ankles."

Lily cried out, and my grip slipped on the camera.

"The water's pulling me deeper, Margaret Anne! I can't fight it, I—"

Lily made an awful choking sound then, and Julian rushed up behind me to grab the camera before it slid from my hands. I stumbled toward Lily, going to my knees and pulling her into my arms. Her body was limp and soft, and I could smell chocolate and coconut in her hair. Her heart thudded, or maybe that was my own pulse leaping into high gear. I smoothed the hair from her face, and after a moment she moaned softly.

Then she opened her eyes.

"Margaret Anne *did* drown in the river," she whispered. "I saw it. I *felt* it."

Lily shivered in my arms, and a familiar pressure expanded in my ears. At the same time I realized the room was turning cooler. A moment ago it had been sweltering, but now I had goose bumps. I glanced up at Julian, but he was looking at the ceiling.

The light fixture was swaying above our heads. It started slowly but gained speed with each swing.

"How's it doing that?" I squeaked.

Julian's mouth sagged open a little, but I couldn't tell if he was afraid or excited. He raised the camera very slowly and aimed it at the fixture. But by the time his thumb found the video button, the swaying had slowed to a halt.

He lowered the camera. "We'd better go."

Julian didn't seem much in the mood to talk on our walk back, so I let him go ahead. There was such a thick layer of weird to this whole deal. Not just weird—*wrong*. But I wasn't exactly sure in what way. Maybe Lily was playing around, and my imagination was running away with me. Or maybe there truly was something dark and strange in the house, something that had lurked for years in silence and was now feeding on our energy. Lily's energy, in particular.

Just as I thought that, she fell in step next to me and slipped her hand in mine.

"Sorry I scared you, Avery."

I stared at her. "I was more worried about *you* being scared."

She shook her head. "I'm not scared of Margaret Anne."

"Really? Because she gives me the creeps."

"I think she's nice."

"If she's so nice, why did she make you go through something scary like *drowning*?"

Lily frowned. "It's not like I was actually about to drown—I was just seeing things from her point of view. She's stuck in that house because something bad happened, but that doesn't mean *she's* bad."

"But why would she make the ceiling fixture sway?"

Lily didn't answer.

I thought back to the movies Julian and I had watched and realized they didn't tell me a whole lot about what it meant to be a ghost. Those movies were more about the secrets and sadness of people who were still alive. So who was I to say that Lily was just a kid and didn't know what she was talking about?

At that moment Lily yawned so big I thought her face might split open.

I squeezed her fingers. "Your dad said you haven't been sleeping well. Are you having nightmares about Margaret Anne, too?"

"I don't think so. It's probably just my bed at the cottage." She turned to me. "Not that it's bad or anything. Just different, you know?"

I nodded. "It always takes me a few nights to get used to the bed in Grandma's attic. It's a little saggy. Meanwhile, Blake got a new mattress this summer because he grew so much over the past year."

"Blake is your brother?"

"Sadly, yes."

Lily's eyes widened. *"Sadly?"*

I sighed. "Oh, I'm mostly teasing. But he has been kind of a jerk lately. He's starting high school in the fall, and all of a sudden he's way too grown-up to hang out with me."

"Julian's starting high school, too, but he still lets me hang around. Probably because he always needs people to be in his movies."

"Or maybe he just likes having you around."

Lily smiled. "Well, I *am* super fabulous."

I pulled her toward me and tickled her ribs. "You're super *deluded!*"

She squirmed and giggled, then threw herself into counterattack. "Tickle fight!"

It felt good to be silly, and Lily was a ferocious little tickler.

She had the advantage of being shorter, meaning her hands were right at the level of my stomach.

"Hey! Are you two coming, or what?"

Julian stood on the crest of the hill, his hands on his hips and a deep scowl on his face. Or maybe he was just squinting in the sun.

"Chill out," I said. "We're just trying to lighten the mood a little."

"I still need to show you that footage from the weekend, Avery. We haven't got all day."

Without waiting for an answer, Julian turned and walked on.

"*Brothers,*" Lily said. "What a pain."

"You said it."

She gave a halfhearted giggle, but we walked the rest of the way in silence.

CHAPTER 18

Once we got back to the cottage, Lily went straight to the living room and curled up on the couch to watch her daddy play guitar. I was hankering for some Weasley cuddling time myself, but there was footage to watch, so I followed Julian upstairs. He pulled the second chair toward the desk and settled himself in front of the keyboard, jiggling his mouse to wake the computer.

"Stupid glare." He rose from the chair to shut the curtains.

Julian's computer desktop was simple and tidy. The wallpaper was plain blue, and there were only four folders, labeled PROJECTS, PHOTOS, FOOTAGE, and BULLIED. The last one stood out to me, though I wasn't sure why.

Then I remembered the clip on Julian's tablet—the one of a school lunchroom.

When Julian sat back down, I pointed at the folder. "What's that?"

He didn't answer right away, and I turned to find him staring at the screen, his jaw tight.

"Is it a movie?" I asked. "I saw a clip with the same title on your tablet. I just, um, happened to be looking at your photos and video clips, and—"

"It's an early project I should have deleted already," he said quickly. "Are you going to bring that tablet back?"

He still wasn't looking at me.

"Julian, were you bullied at school or something?"

"No, I wasn't." He cleared his throat. "Can we move on? Before we get to the shots from yesterday, I want to show you something." He opened the footage folder and clicked on a file titled DRAFT1 to expand it to full screen. "I've been playing around with the opening of our film. I put some still shots together and changed them all to black and white, and I applied a filter to make it look a little aged."

He clicked Play and an image faded in—a wide shot of the pasture with the old cow barn standing a little left of center. That transitioned to a shot of the cattail pond, which looked more artistic than I would have expected in the grainy black-and-white filter. The next image was Hilliard House—a daytime shot taken at a low angle so that it looked proud and tall. That faded into the nighttime photo he'd shown me the week before, with the light in the window. He'd lined the images up almost perfectly, and the transition made my scalp tingle. A title appeared below the house in pale letters that glowed and flickered:

GHOSTLIGHT

BY

JULIAN WAYNE

The whole screen faded to black again.

"Wow," I said.

"Do you like it?"

"Um, yeah. It's cool, but it also gives me the creeps. Is that going to be the movie's title?"

"Maybe." He backed the scene up and paused at the title frame. "It's a theater term. Supposedly every theater has a ghost, and long ago people started leaving a stage light on to keep the ghosts happy. You know, in case they wanted to perform when no one was around. Neat, huh?"

Before I could respond, he pulled up another file.

"Here's the footage I wanted to show you."

It was a scene from Margaret Anne's room. Lily sat on the braided rug holding the tarnished silver frame. The doll sat next to her, propped against the bed frame.

"She made me pick the mouse droppings out of that thing's belly," Julian murmured.

Lily straightened the doll's legs and then focused on the photograph. "Margaret Anne," she called softly. "Are you there?"

Lily's body rocked gently as she continued to stare at the photograph, a lot like what I'd seen earlier that day. She called out twice more, each time sounding a little more desperate, and then her body stilled. She looked up, eyes wide. The camera zoomed in so far that I could see the fat pupils of her eyes.

"I see you there," Lily said.

Heat flushed my cheeks, traveling all the way to the roots of my hair. I wasn't afraid, exactly. My heart was thumping and my face was hot because I felt off-kilter, as if everything around me had tilted.

At that point, the camera pulled back and panned to the right, moving Lily to the left of the frame. The doll sat at the center. On the right was the empty space Lily was staring at. I stared, too, trying to see what she saw.

"Of course I'll be your friend," Lily said. "Do you want to play?"

She put the photo down and pretended to set a table for tea and cookies, all the while chattering away . . . to nobody.

"Does this remind you of anything?" Julian asked.

"Huh?"

"She's talking to someone in Hilliard House."

The back of my neck started prickling so bad I had to hunch my shoulders.

Julian turned back to the computer screen and pointed. "Now, watch closely."

All I saw was Lily talking as she mimed pouring tea from an imaginary pot into an imaginary cup.

"Did you see it?"

I shook my head. "What am I supposed to be seeing?"

"Watch the space next to Lily." He paused the video and moved it back several frames. "Try to look where she's looking."

This time I concentrated, and at the point where Lily raised the pretend cup to her lips, something flickered in that space where Julian had told me to look. The space where Margaret Anne was supposed to be.

"Did you see it that time?"

"I saw *something*. Or maybe I just blinked."

"I'll pause it," he said, backing up the scene again.

Once again we watched Lily pouring her invisible tea. Just as she had brought her own invisible cup two inches from her lips, Julian paused the video. This time I could see the wispy thing hanging in the air across from Lily. It wasn't a person, but it was *something*. Like a puff of steam.

I turned to him. "Are you saying that's Margaret Anne's ghost?"

"Well . . . I just think it's cool. We could be making a ghost movie in a house that's actually haunted." His eyes gleamed. "It would explain what your brother saw all those years ago."

I stared at the wispy thing on the screen. "Why can't I see her *now*?"

"Maybe you're too old. Maybe she can only show herself to people her age. That's why Lily can see her and we can't."

My shoulders were bunching up again. "I'm not going back there again."

"Avery, we have to go back. One more time is all, I promise. I need to finish the movie, and maybe we'll get a clearer shot of the . . . whatever it is. Can you imagine how cool that would be? We could be famous."

"I don't know. I need to think about this."

He shook his head. "There's no time. Your grandma's selling the place. If we don't do it tomorrow, we may never have the chance again."

Mom cooked supper that night—her way of making up with Grandma after the church Communion incident. Blake and I loved her cheese enchiladas with blue corn chips and homemade salsa, but Grandma's mouth tightened as she picked at her plate.

"Is this what they call Tex-Mex?" she muttered. "A little bit of ground beef wouldn't have gone amiss."

Mom took the high road by ignoring her. "I was thinking tomorrow would be the perfect day for our trek to the lake. Forecast looks great."

I set my fork down. "Julian and I are supposed to finish filming tomorrow."

"Well . . ." Mom frowned. "I'm going with Grandma to the Realtor on Wednesday. There's a solid offer on Hilliard House and the buyers want to move quickly. Maybe that would be a good day for you guys to finish?"

"I don't need your help, Maddie," Grandma said. "I've managed without you before. You three can go to the lake on Wednesday if you like."

"But I want to help, Mama."

"Well, in that case . . ." Grandma smiled.

Mom turned to me. "So, swimming at the lake tomorrow? Are we settled?"

I nodded and tried to smile. "I'll just call Julian."

The thing was . . . if Grandma was meeting with the Realtor on Wednesday, I needed to have the key back tomorrow, just to be safe. That meant we'd never finish the film.

So why did I feel more than a little relieved?

After supper I took Grandma's phone upstairs to call Julian.

"We'll just have to do it tonight," he said after I'd explained. "Actually, that would be even better."

"Tonight? Mom won't let me. I'm supposed to be in bed by eight-thirty."

"Then sneak out."

The words were like fingers clamping around my throat.

"Avery, are you there?"

"Yes," I croaked.

"It's no big deal. I do this sort of thing all the time. We can meet at eleven and they'll all be asleep. Your mom and grandma will never even know. Remember what I told you about artists and taking risks?"

"But—"

"Are you afraid of being in that house at night?"

"Well . . . *yeah.*"

"Perfect. It'll look great on film."

CHAPTER 19

The darkness was loud and hungry as I walked to Hilliard House. Crickets and katydids thickened the air with their chirps. Mosquitoes buzzed in my ears. The humidity draped around me like a damp curtain—all day it had looked like it might rain, but only a few drops fell. The clouds blacked out the stars, and God only knew what lurked in the shadows behind the trees.

Julian had said he'd be waiting on the front steps of Hilliard House. The flashlight didn't throw off much light, so I didn't see him until I was a few feet from the house.

"You freak," I said. "Why are you sitting there in the dark?"

"I like it." His foot tapped the bottom step. "It puts me in the mood for filming."

He had that jittery thing going on again. Plus he looked super freaky with a lamp strapped on his head, like he was a cave explorer or something.

"Where's Lily?" I asked.

"She's sick. But we can work without her. I'll just get some footage of you, and then we should be done."

I flashed my light on the house, which oozed gloom in the

darkness. "But what's the story going to be? I haven't exactly seen a beginning, middle, or end to this thing."

"Trust me. I know what I'm doing."

He stood so quickly that I took a step back. He was wearing that strange T-shirt again—the one with the cartoon outline of a man's profile.

"All right," I said. "Who *is* that on your shirt? Another film director?"

He sighed. "Seriously? It's Alfred Hitchcock."

The name sounded familiar.

"*Rear Window*?" Julian said. "*Dial M for Murder*? How about *Psycho*?"

He looked like a psycho in the glow of my flashlight, but I held back from saying so. "Seems like I've heard of those movies."

"People called Hitchcock the Master of Suspense. He made all sorts of spooky movies, but he never actually made a ghost film." Julian lifted the backpack and slung it over his shoulder. "I don't want to turn on my headlamp until we get inside. You go ahead—I already unlocked the door."

"You're going to give me that key back when we're done tonight, right? I keep forgetting to ask for it."

"Of course you'll get it back. Did you think I was going to steal it?"

He stood on the top step with his arms crossed, as if he was trying to hold himself together. Maybe his dad had been right to ask him about his meds.

I summoned a calm, grown-up sort of voice. "Julian, are you okay?"

Even in the weak glow of my flashlight I could see the

hurt in his eyes, and I started to apologize. But then he clasped his hands and stared at them for a long moment, breathing deeply like Mom had told me to do. Finally he raised his eyes to mine. "I'm totally okay. I think . . . I'm just excited to shoot this last scene. And I can't do it without you, Avery."

My chest swelled a little at that. "All right. Tell me what to do."

"I'll follow you in and get the camera set up. I want to do one last trip upstairs."

"Without Lily?"

"I want to focus on *your* experience of Margaret Anne's room." He shrugged out of his backpack and stepped aside for me. "Go on in."

Something strange happened when I walked through that door. A feeling washed over me—cold but also prickly, like heat. It stopped me in my tracks.

Julian came up behind me. "Will you move so I can get inside?"

I took a few steps forward. As soon as he'd shut the door, he turned his headlamp on and started working the settings on his camera as if nothing had happened.

"Did you feel that?"

He didn't look up. "Feel what?"

"It was like a wave crashing into me." I rubbed my arms. "I still feel it—hot and cold at the same time, like when you have the flu."

He raised his head, shining the light in my eyes. "You look a little pale. Maybe you're coming down with what Lily has." He snapped the microphone into place. "By the way, pale is perfect for this scene."

When I stepped toward the staircase, the feeling eased up a bit. "I think it was coming from the parlor," I said. "But it wasn't like that before."

"Forget about that room," said Julian. "It's not interesting on film." He moved to stand in the dining room doorway. "Go back outside and walk through the door, but take your time. And try to look a little confused."

"I *am* confused. What am I supposed to be doing?"

"You're looking for Lily. You think she might be in the house. I'm going to film you going up the stairs to Margaret Anne's room."

I shook my head. "But Lily's not here."

"That's the point. I know how the movie ends."

"How? I don't even know how it started. You never talked about the *story* with me."

He blew his breath out impatiently. "This movie is about two sisters. The younger sister, played by Lily, can sense things in the house that the older sister can't."

"And?"

"One night the younger sister disappears. Your character comes to the house to look for her. But she's not here. Margaret Anne has taken her. The younger sister disappears into the house, lost forever."

My heart lurched. "You mean the house swallows her up or something? There's no body?"

"That's what I'm thinking. I mean, we don't exactly have the budget for a death scene." He held up the camera.

"Okay, if you're done with the twenty questions, we should get started. Come through the front door again. Take your time and I'll follow. Maybe you could call out to Lily when you get halfway up the stairs—I think that would be cool."

"So we're using real names?"

"Lily will love it."

I looked back at the door. I didn't want that wave crashing into me again, but at least after tonight I wouldn't have to deal with it. I walked out the door, closed it, and after a pause reached for the knob. It didn't want to turn at first, but when I leaned against the door, it turned easily. I braced myself, but the wave of queasiness was even more intense this time.

Out of the corner of my eye I saw Julian give me the thumbs-up. My suffering must have looked good on film. Leaving the door open, I pushed through until I reached the foot of the stairs.

I could feel the camera staring at me.

"Lily?" My voice was scratchy.

I put my hand on the banister and pulled myself up the stairs, one step at a time. All I had to do was go to Margaret Anne's room and act like I couldn't find Lily. Then I'd make a big scaredy face at the camera, and maybe that would be enough for Julian.

"Stop there and don't move an inch," said Julian. "I want to go to the top and film you from a high angle."

To make me look small and helpless.

When he got to the top and gestured for me to follow, I took each step slowly, pausing two-thirds of the way. "Lily, are you up there?"

I heard something then. Just the barest whisper of a sound,

like a hiss or a splash. I looked straight at the camera, but Julian didn't stop. Maybe he hadn't heard it. I started down the hallway toward Margaret Anne's room, but paused at the bathroom. The door had always been wide open before. Now it was partly closed. I pointed my flashlight through the gap and saw the bathtub.

The last time we were here, the tub had been dark with dirt and rust stains.

Now I could see water in it.

I turned back to Julian. "What's going on?"

With his left hand he pointed at the bathroom door and made the winding-film gesture.

Keep going.

My heart pounded a little faster as I stepped toward the door and pushed it wider. The tub was deep, and the water came all the way to the top. Some of it had splashed over the side, leaving puddles on the floor.

I could feel Julian behind me, so I took another step toward the tub. A coil of dark hair floated to the surface. I moved closer and saw the flower print of a dress with the skirt floating up. Bare arms, thin and brown, were wrapped around the china doll.

"Lily!"

I stumbled to the edge of the tub. She lay at the bottom, her hair reaching up to the surface like pondweed. The doll's pink skirt and petticoat lifted to reveal the strangely tiny feet. Its painted eyes stared. Lily's green eyes were wide open, too—glassy and lifeless like the doll's. Her lips were parted, but no bubbles rose to the surface.

I turned to Julian, who was still filming.

"What are you doing? Help me get her out!"

Julian seemed frozen in place. I couldn't see his face under that crazy headlamp, but I knew shock could do that to a person. My own arms and legs felt heavy, like I was moving through a nightmare. I dropped the flashlight and turned back to Lily.

She was so small. All I had to do was place my hands behind her neck and lift her up. Maybe that would shake some sense into Julian. He knew everything—surely he would know how to squeeze the water out of her lungs and get her breathing again.

I reached toward her with shaking hands.

In a rush and splashing of water, Lily sat straight up and stared at me with those wide, dead eyes. Her mouth opened and an inhuman sound came out—a shriek like nothing I'd ever heard in this world.

I reared back, gasping for breath as my heart vaulted into my throat. My hands scrambled for something to break my fall, but there was nothing except slick tile.

The last thing I saw before my head hit the wall behind me was Julian still holding the camera.

CHAPTER 20

My head pounded.

I pressed my fingers against the back of my skull.

No blood.

I opened one eye. Lily crouched in the tub, clutching the doll to her chest and shivering. I was shivering, too, and I didn't have even a drop of water on me.

"Avery." She wiped water out of her eyes and pointed at me. "I think you peed yourself."

I opened my other eye to take in the stain that trailed darkly down my pant leg.

Lily grabbed the edge of the tub to push herself up. "I can hold my breath a long time. Julian said it would be perfect for the movie."

All I could do was stare. She was cold and wet and very much alive.

"I never saw anyone so scared." Lily seemed pleased with herself as she said it. But then her lower lip started to tremble. "Julian said you had to face your fear. That it would be good for you." She turned to her brother, who'd finally put the camera down. "Right?"

He said nothing, his face still in shadow under the head-lamp that shined right in my eyes.

I scrambled to my knees. "You *planned* this?"

He lowered his head, finally turning the light away from me.

"I asked you a question!"

"This was a key scene," he said quietly. "I needed an authentic reaction from you."

"I thought Lily was *dead*!"

He glanced at his sister. "She's a good actress. It had to seem real."

I turned to Lily. "You've been acting this whole time, haven't you? *Pretending* about Margaret Anne."

Lily swallowed hard.

I faced Julian again. "I know this was all your idea. You messed with that photo of the house, didn't you? You added that light in the window just to get me spooked. And then, when I told you something personal and private, you used it. You got your sister to pretend she was speaking to a ghost, and you added that image to the movie."

"No, that's not it—"

"You're such a jerk. You made the door slam shut and the light fixture sway." My head pounded with anger now. "I . . . nearly had . . . a heart attack. I might have a concussion!"

Lily rubbed her eyes, sniffling and shivering. The doll's head lolled dangerously, ready to break off at any moment. Lily was a small, crying child who probably hadn't meant any harm, but my heart was dead cold at the moment. Nasty, angry words were stacking up behind my clenched lips.

I opened my mouth and set them free.

"Julian, you're nuts. You must be off your meds to do something like this."

His chin dropped.

"You should be locked away like your mother."

His fingers tightened around the camera strap. Then he took a step toward me.

I struggled to stand. "Don't you dare touch me!"

Just as the words came out of my mouth, the bulb on Julian's forehead shattered. He flew back, slamming against the opposite wall.

"Jules!" cried Lily, dropping the doll.

I scooped up my flashlight and pointed it at him. His body slid down the wall, camera clattering as it hit the tile floor. He lifted a finger to his cheek and it came away streaked with blood.

Lily shrieked.

I turned the light on her. "Shut up!"

A tear spilled out of her eye. "When you pointed the flashlight . . . there was a shadow in the mirror. A man's shadow!"

That strange pressure filled my ears, making them ache, and I gritted my teeth to keep from screaming back at her. "That's it. Seriously, you can quit the whole act now, because I'm done with this."

After one last glance at Julian, I stumbled out of the bathroom, leaving them to fend for themselves in the dark.

I didn't cry.

I didn't swear or fuss.

I didn't feel much at all.

All that mattered on the walk back to Grandma's was getting inside quietly, cleaning up, and going to bed. My brain couldn't handle much else.

I'd meant to get in through the carport door, which I'd left unlocked because it was the farthest from Grandma's bedroom, but some idiot had locked it. Probably Mom. She wasn't an idiot, but she *was* a restless busybody at night.

I walked around to the rear of the house to check the utility room door.

Locked.

I flinched as something soft tickled my leg. Weasley stood at my feet, his tail curling around my ankle.

"Oh, Weasley." I knelt down to rub his arched back and scratch his chin. He rumbled his appreciation. "What do I do now?"

He stared at me for a moment, his eyes dark and glistening. Then he slipped through the cat flap in the utility room door.

"Lot of good that does me," I muttered.

Only the breezeway door remained, so I returned to the front of the house. Opening the screen door as quietly as possible, I said a little prayer before twisting the knob on the inner door.

No luck.

I eased the screen door shut and swiped at a sting on my ankle. My bug spray was officially starting to wear off.

Options? None. Well, just one, but it would come at a price. I made my way around to the west side of the house and tapped on the music room window.

No answer.

I tapped louder. *Please, God, don't let Blake be plugged into his stupid music.*

I'd clenched my fist to knock when the window opened.

"What the heck, Avery?" Blake's hair was smashed on one side and sticking up on the other. "Are you crazy?"

"I'm locked out. Let me in the carport door."

He groaned. "I'm not walking past Grandma's bedroom and all the way across the house to let you in."

I swatted at another mosquito. "Then let me through the breezeway door. But *please* be quiet."

"What do I get for being quiet?"

"I don't care. Whatever you want, Blake. I'm tired."

"I've heard a life of crime can be pretty exhausting."

I'd reached the top step when I saw a beam of light through the glass. Blake was using the flashlight function on his phone. He unlocked the door without too much noise and even held the screen door open as I slipped through.

I gripped the knob, taking the door's weight as it softly clicked shut. Now all I had to do was make it through the living room without the floor creaking and I'd be home free.

Blake sniffed. "What's that smell?"

He flashed the light at me.

I couldn't help looking down. The stain was drying, but it still stood out clearly against the lighter fabric of my pants.

When I met his gaze again, he rolled his eyes in disgust.

Something inside me snapped, and the wave of tears dammed up in my skull chose that moment to break free. Tears spilled down my cheeks, and I gasped and hiccuped, which only brought more tears and hiccups.

"Jeez, Avery, what happened?"

"Ju-Julian tricked me. He and Lily sc-scared me on purpose."

"What were you doing out at *night*? Oh, never mind, you'd better calm down or Mom's going to hear you."

"I p-peed my pants."

"Yeah, I see that."

"They totally scammed me, Blake. A film geek and a little girl." I wiped my nose with the back of my hand. "No wonder you hate me. I'm such a loser."

His shoulders sank. "Aw, I don't hate you. You really are crazy tonight."

"I'm serious, I—"

The floor creaked in the living room, and both our heads snapped toward the doorway.

Mom stood in the light of Blake's phone lamp, her hair wild with sleep.

"What on earth are you two doing?"

CHAPTER 21

"You're going to wake Grandma, and then we'll all be in trouble," Mom whispered. "Blake, you need to go back to bed."

"Fine with me," he muttered.

"Avery, I'll speak with you in the sewing room."

I crept through the living and dining rooms, dodging all the creaky spots in the floor. The shock of seeing Mom had dried my tears right up, and a strange calm had settled over me. Once we were inside Grandma's sewing room, Mom carefully closed the door behind us and turned on the lamp.

"All right, young lady. What's going on?"

"Nothing."

"You do know I question people for a living, right?"

I shrugged.

"Okay, have it your way." She gestured at my clothes. "You're fully dressed and you've been outside. Were you with that boy, Avery? Do I have to worry about that sort of stuff already with you?"

"What stuff?" My whole head felt hot. "Jeez, Mom. I don't like him that way."

Her shoulders softened. "I'm still waiting for an explanation."

"We were filming. Julian wanted to film at night."

"Why at night?"

I looked down at my hands.

"Avery?"

"It's a ghost movie, Mom," I said. "And Julian needed a scary scene . . . so he scared me."

She leaned back. "What in the world gave you the idea to make a ghost movie? You hate scary stuff."

"It wasn't *my* idea. Julian is obsessed with Joshua Hilliard and that old house. He decided on a ghost movie when he found out Joshua's daughter drowned in the 1937 flood."

"Margaret Anne didn't drown."

"What?"

She waved the question away. "Where were you filming, exactly?"

"Inside Hilliard House."

Her eyes widened. "How did you get in?"

"I . . . borrowed Grandma's key."

She stared at me for a long moment. "Avery, when did my baby girl become a thief?" Her voice was low and flat, which meant she was furious. "When did she decide it was okay to sneak around and *lie*?"

A minute ago all I wanted was for this lecture to be over. For me to change out of my smelly pants into pajamas and fall into bed. But now my blood was pounding again.

"Maybe I learned to lie from you."

She flinched. "What? I've never lied to you."

I crossed my arms. "I want to go to bed."

"I don't think so. If you're going to say that to me, you need to explain yourself."

We played the staring game. I dug in, ready to stare back until she caved and let me go to bed. But hardly a minute passed before my eyes started burning and my leg twitched, and I just couldn't keep from blinking.

"Well, Avery?"

"I found an old photo of you," I finally said.

"And?"

"I was looking through Grandpa's albums for pictures of the people who lived at Hilliard House. I got to the album with you as a little girl, and as a teenager. You never told us much about that time, Mom."

"There wasn't much to tell. You know I felt pretty lonely on this hill."

"Well, you weren't as alone as I thought. That photo I found . . . Grandpa had folded it in half. But I saw part of a hand on the left side. So . . . I took it out of the album."

Her face crumpled. "Oh, Avery."

"How could you forget to tell me you were married? We could have had a real daddy, but you pushed this man away and never told us a thing about him. Or never told *me*, anyway."

She stood silent for a long time, her face drooping. She'd always seemed young for her age. I mean, she was older than most moms I knew, but she still dressed young and took care of herself. In that moment, though, it was easy to see how she might look when she was Grandma's age.

Finally she moved Grandma's sewing chair toward me. "Sit."

I did as told, watching her as she rolled the desk chair toward me and sat.

"I didn't tell you about Rick because I didn't want to confuse you. I didn't want you to think he might have been your dad. Blake figured it out after Grandma slipped up last summer. He wanted to tell you, but I told him you were still too young."

"I wasn't. I'm *not*."

"Fine. What do you want to know about him?"

I thought for a moment. "I guess . . . I just want to know why you couldn't stay married to him."

"All right. But it's better if I start from the beginning." She cleared her throat. "I married Rick when I was nineteen. I'd always meant to go to college, but he was my high school sweetheart and he kind of swept me off my feet. And, honestly, I think Grandma and Grandpa were pleased, because it meant I would stay in Carver County instead of going far away."

"Did he hurt you or something?"

She shook her head. "He was a nice enough guy. But . . . his world was so small. He was happy staying in the county, working a shift, and coming home to watch TV at night. He didn't want to go to college, and he didn't want me to go, either. I wanted to learn and travel. To take risks and grow. Rick just wanted a quiet, safe, simple life." She ran both hands through her hair. "It was a mutual decision to end it."

"And then you moved to Texas."

"I went to UT and worked at the same time. I applied for every scholarship and grant I could find. Even if Mama and Daddy had the money for tuition—which they didn't—I wasn't about to ask them to pay for my leaving. I've told you all this before."

"I know, but I want to hear it all—*including* the stuff you've kept from me."

She nodded. "After working for the university for a few years, I decided to go to law school. I worked harder than I've ever worked in my life. I've been working hard ever since."

"But you must have met another man you liked along the way. Someone to make a family with."

She smiled and used her Southern voice. "Why, Avery May, I never knew you were so conventional."

I wasn't exactly sure what that meant, but it didn't sound good. "How am I conventional?"

"It just means going with what everyone else thinks is normal. Maybe you've been watching too much *Little House* with Grandma." She took my hand. "I certainly didn't expect to be having this conversation at Grandma's."

"I'm not a baby, Mom." I took a deep breath. "Do you not like men anymore?"

She placed my hand on her palm and stroked my fingers. "It's not that simple. After Rick and I split up, I focused on *my* dreams. And I worked long hours for years. I was friendly with people at school and work, but I didn't have a whole lot of *friends*. Does that make sense?"

"Yeah, I guess."

"I always knew I wanted kids, but I couldn't even think about it until I made partner at the firm. I never wanted to have to tell you or Blake that I couldn't pay for your college tuition."

"I get it, Mom."

"Good. So . . . by the time I made partner, I was in my mid-thirties—already at that iffy age of getting pregnant, and there was no life partner in sight. I'd been too busy for friends, let alone boyfriends. But I wanted a family so badly, Avery. Well, I wanted *kids*. I wasn't so sure about another husband."

"So you just bought what you needed from a donor." I couldn't help cringing, even though I could tell it hurt her feelings.

She took both my hands. "I was running out of time, and I couldn't make the love of my life appear out of thin air. I'm sorry."

I stared at our clasped hands.

"Avery, look at me. I know I didn't do this the traditional way, but we've had a good life, haven't we? We've had so much love." She placed my hands back on my lap. "I didn't realize how much not having a father bothered you."

"It's always bothered me," I whispered. "Ever since I started school, anyway."

"We're a different sort of family, and at your age that's hard. But, honey, even with *one* parent you get more love than a lot of kids get. Will you try to remember that?"

My eyes were welling up again. Part of me was still angry, but deep in my belly was a coil of shame that twisted wider and wider.

"I will," I finally said.

"Good." Mom shifted in her chair. "Now, your first task is to return that key to Grandma."

"Are you going to tell her everything?"

She held my gaze for a long moment. "Honesty is important to me—you know that. If she asks me a direct question about it, I'll have to tell her. But for now she's probably better off not knowing about your antics at Hilliard House. If you give me the key now, I'll put it back the first chance I get."

My chest sank. "I . . . um, don't have it. Julian does."

"Well, you'd better get it, my girl. Grandma will be looking for that key soon—you know we have a meeting with the Realtor—and there's no way I can protect you if she learns what you've done with it." She stood. "Now go clean up and put those clothes in the hamper. *Quietly.*"

CHAPTER 22

I slept a dark, dreamless sleep and woke to a fat beam of light coming through the window. Ordinarily Grandma couldn't abide slugabeds, but Mom must have convinced her to leave me alone. By the time I stumbled downstairs, she and Blake were coming in from the garden.

"Hey, sleepyhead!" Mom tousled my hair. "We made a quick job of it this morning. Need to head to the lake before it gets too hot."

I waited for Blake to complain about having to do my work, but for once he kept his mouth shut. Actually, he looked at me almost like he was *concerned.* It creeped me out a little.

"What?" I rubbed my cheek. "Do I have slobber on my face or something?"

"No." He glanced back at the kitchen. "Are you, um, okay?"

I nodded.

"That Julian kid is bad news."

"I'm getting the key back today. Mom knows everything."

"Yeah, she told me." The corner of his mouth lifted. "Guess you've foiled my evil blackmail scheme."

"Are you guys ready for a quick breakfast?" Mom called from the kitchen. "We need to hit the road."

"Get your suit," Blake said. "Mom's already packed the towels and lunch. She says you can get the key after we come home." He turned toward the kitchen.

"Hey, Blake?"

He glanced back at me. "Yeah?"

"Sorry . . . about last night. And about missing the garden work."

He turned to face me, crossing his arms. "Oh, believe me, I'm working up a new and elaborate plan for extortion."

I stared at him for a moment, my mouth hanging open. Then I saw the twinkle in his eyes.

"Right," I said. "Just remember two can play at that game, Mr. Summer-Reading Fail."

Having a day like old times—the three of us talking over one another as we drove to the lake, me and Blake horsing around in the water—helped push the whole dark business of Julian out of my mind for a while. Mom must have asked Blake to be extra nice. Any other time that would have ruined things for me, but after such a crazy night it was pretty cool.

The magic started to wear off on the drive back. I was worn out from swimming and too much sun, and once we hit the gravel driveway to Grandma's house, the darkness and dread settled right back in. It would've been so much easier if I never had to see Julian again. If Mom would just get the key for me, I could fold those memories away and shut the drawer on them.

I sent her a fragile, tormented look when I climbed out of the car, but she was having none of it.

"Go jump in the shower, Avery. You still have a job to do, and it needs to happen before supper."

"But, Mom, it'll take a while for my hair to dry and all—"

"Your hair can dry on the way. Get a move on."

Half an hour later I was crunching gravel on the walk down to Hollyhock Cottage, Julian's tablet in my hands and a wet ponytail dripping down my back. The hope that Curtis Wayne would be in a baking mood pushed me through those final steps up to the door, but when I heard the sounds of guitar strumming *and* singing, I knew there'd be no cookies or conversation to ease things along.

I knocked lightly on the door. After a moment it opened and Lily peered out. The shadows under her green eyes told me she was still having trouble sleeping.

"Hey, Avery," she said softly.

I straightened. "I came to get the key to Hilliard House." I glanced past her toward the living room. "But I can come back if this is a bad time."

"It's okay. Dad's writing songs now, so he doesn't really hear us anymore. We have to stand right in front of him and shout to get his attention." She opened the door wide. "Julian has your key." She turned to lead me toward the staircase, but after one step she paused. "Avery, I'm sorry. About . . . you know."

I guess if I was a nice person—a Christianly person—I would have smiled and told her it was okay. Instead the heat came to my face, and I wondered if she was just messing with me again. She was a little actress, after all, and she'd well and truly tricked me last night.

"I just need the key, Lily. Otherwise I'll be in even bigger trouble than I'm already in."

She nodded with a sad little sigh—still acting?—and led me up the stairs. Julian's door was shut, so she knocked three times, paused, and then knocked twice. After a moment I heard footsteps on the wood floor and the door opened.

Julian looked tired, too, and the cut on his cheek was puffy. His whole body seemed to droop when his eyes met mine.

I handed him the tablet. "Now give me the key back."

Julian set the tablet on his bed and walked to his desk. Lily sidled out of the room, but not before one last glance at me. She sure had the "pitiful child" act nailed. I turned back to see Julian reaching for a small plastic box, which he popped open and shook until he saw what he wanted. He pulled out the key. Then he turned in his chair and held it out to me.

He was going to make me walk to him and take it. Without even saying a word.

I hoped my face didn't look as red hot as it felt.

"So that's it?" I finally asked. The words came out kind of choked.

He shrugged.

"You don't have anything to say to me? I think you owe me an apology."

"I'm sorry, I guess."

It came out more as a sigh than a heartfelt statement.

I snatched the key from his hand. "You guess? You *guess*

you're sorry? You used me, lied to me, made *me* lie and steal, and then you scared the pee out of me. *Literally.* And all you can say is 'I'm sorry, I guess'?"

"Are you done yet? I have other projects to work on."

I would have stormed out at that moment, except . . . his eyes glistened suspiciously.

"It wasn't all lies," said a small voice from the hallway.

Julian groaned. "Lily, how many times have I told you not to listen at the door?"

Lily popped her head around the doorframe. "But she needs to know."

"Know what?" I said.

"That we didn't make *all* of it up."

My right hand curled into a fist. "You guys just don't stop, do you? Mom told me Margaret Anne Hilliard didn't die in the flood. She didn't even drown, so I know Julian made that up."

"It was a working theory," he said.

I narrowed my eyes at Lily. "And you. Pretending to speak to Margaret Anne just to freak me out."

"I just . . . well, I wanted to talk with her so bad, I guess my imagination sort of filled in the gaps." She bit her lip. "But I saw and heard things, Avery. *Felt* things. I don't know if it was Margaret Anne or not, 'cause I know it was a man's shadow in the mirror last night."

I turned back to Julian. "Are you two still trying to scam me?"

He shook his head. "Lily says there's something there. And I believe her."

"Yeah, whatever."

"Seriously, Avery. You may still think I rigged the door and light fixture, but you can't believe that I threw myself against the wall and exploded my own headlamp."

He was trying to make *me* feel guilty for accusing them of lying, which made no sense at all. So I just turned and walked out of the room.

Lily crept behind me like a shadow as I made my way down the stairs. Mr. Wayne sat in the living room, holding the music stand with one hand and scribbling something on the paper with the other. The guitar sat in his lap, glossy and smug. I wondered if Julian ever wished he could throw that thing in a gully.

I was halfway down the hall when Lily called my name.

"What is it now?" I asked.

Lily pulled the framed photograph of Margaret Anne from her back pocket. The silver gleamed as though she'd polished it. She placed it in my hand, still warm from being so close to her body.

"I took it from the house," she said. "I just . . . I wanted her to be real."

CHAPTER 23

I found Mom and Blake sitting on folding chairs under the oak tree, sipping iced sun tea. They'd both showered, and Mom's hair was curling as it dried. When I handed her the key, she gave my hand a squeeze.

"Don't look so grim, sweetie. Now we can put all this behind us."

"I know. Julian just . . . well, he and Lily are still messing with my head."

"Do I need to talk to that boy's father?" Mom gripped the plastic armrests like she was going to stand.

I shook my head. "The last thing I want is for you to get up in Curtis Wayne's face."

"You were crazy upset last night, Avery," said Blake.

"I don't want to talk about it anymore," I said. "Think I'll take a walk."

I made straight for the copper beech tree and crawled beneath its branches. After settling against the trunk, I took deep breaths of cool air and listened to the leaves whisper in the breeze. All I wanted was to slide back into the woodsy magic of Kingdom—just for a little bit—but it seemed more cramped than usual under the leafy canopy. Plus, something in my pocket was poking my behind. I pulled out the framed photograph and studied the faces of those two girls. Then I turned the photo over and shifted the little metal pieces so I could take the cardboard backing off.

Someone had written names in sprawling cursive on the back of the photo.

Margaret Anne & Aileen

I considered their faces again. Margaret Anne's dandelion hair had settled into curls by that time. She smiled, but didn't look directly at the camera. Little Aileen, all pointy knees and elbows, looked straight at me from out of the photograph. She had the sort of face that smiled from the eyes as well as the mouth. Her dress seemed too big for her. I wondered if she was still alive, and if she might have anything useful to tell us about Hilliard House.

Lily says there's something there, Julian had said. *And I believe her.*

Despite what they'd done to me, I believed her, too. The first day we went inside the house I'd felt that warmth in the parlor. But once we'd focused on Margaret Anne, the place turned weird and dark.

Just as I put the photograph back in its frame, the branches rustled. A hand parted the leaves and Blake peered through.

"Can I come in?" he asked.

I shoved the frame back in my pocket. "Did Mom send you after me?"

"No."

"Why are you here, then?"

"I like this tree, too, you know." He picked at a shriveled leaf.

"Come on in, I guess."

Blake pushed the branch to the side and squeezed through. "It's smaller under here than I remembered." He sat down—not quite next to me, but not too far. "I've been thinking about Kingdom. Do you want to work on Princess Etheline's wedding? I've had a few ideas for the treaty."

My heart made a little leap in my chest. "That's nice of you, Blake, but—"

"I'm not trying to be nice."

I glanced at him. "All I meant to say is . . . you were right before. Kingdom's not the same anymore."

After a moment he nodded.

"I need different stories now," I said.

"Yeah, like what?"

I braced myself. "Maybe . . . something to do with Hilliard House."

"Jeez, Avery. Are you crazy? Just leave that place alone."

I was this close to swearing back at him. But he was partly right. I did sound a little nutty. "It's just . . . the house won't leave *me* alone."

"What's that supposed to mean?"

"There's something there. I felt it. Julian and Lily felt it. Heck, even Grandma says she felt it a long time ago, and that must be why she freaked out when she found me there."

"What kind of 'something' are you talking about?"

I couldn't look at him. "Something . . . ghostly?"

The seconds ticked by, and he didn't say anything. When the silence grew to a roaring in my ears, I risked a peek at him.

I expected him to look disgusted, but he seemed thoughtful instead.

"Well, it sure seemed like you were talking to *someone* that time I heard you in the house," he said.

I perked up. "Did it sound like I was talking to a girl my age?"

"I don't know, maybe? You were very cheerful and chatty." He frowned. "Except, you weren't giggling or talking about make-believe stuff, as far as I could tell. It was like someone was asking you questions, and you were replying very politely."

"I wish I could remember. It's going to keep bugging me until I figure it out."

"What if you did remember? What difference would it make?"

I sighed. "I don't know. The thing is, I can't stop thinking about the cemetery."

Blake shook his head. "Now, that's just creepy."

"There's a real mystery here, Blake. Just give me a second to explain."

He shifted, and I was afraid he was getting up to leave. But he was just turning himself to face me. "All right. I'm listening."

"Okay . . . the last owner of Hilliard House is buried in Clearview Cemetery, but in a different grave from his wife and daughter. Why? The daughter died when she was seven, and nobody seems to know exactly how. Who was I talking to at Hilliard House that night you heard me? And why does the house seem angry now?"

"Uh . . . how can a house be angry?"

"Well, last night things got out of hand." I told him about the exploding headlamp, and how something seemed to push Julian against the wall. "Lily'd been making a big show of talking to the ghost of Margaret Anne, and then she even pretended to be drowned in the bathtub—"

"She did *what*? That's pretty sick."

"I know, but she did it because Julian thought Margaret Anne drowned in the flood of 1937. They were trying to scare me for the movie. What I'm trying to say is . . . maybe it made the house, or whatever's inside the house, mad. Or even *hurt*."

Blake shook his head again, as if he couldn't quite take it all in. I didn't want to push it, so I shut my mouth and let my thoughts wander.

Julian and Lily had made up a story about Hilliard House, but now I wanted to know the truth about Margaret Anne and Joshua Hilliard. Grandma had told me some things, but Mom had actually spent time with Mr. Hilliard. If she'd known Margaret Anne didn't drown, she must know other things, too. All I had to do was ask. And maybe I could write it all down and make a story out of it. It'd be nothing like Kingdom, no magic or adventure, but this story would have to do with *my* family, and it would be real. Mom was being funny when she made that crack about me being an investigative reporter, but maybe I really could be a detective uncovering the facts. Maybe that was what the house really wanted—just for someone to tell the truth.

I sat up straight. "I want to ask Mom some questions about Joshua Hilliard, but first I need to go back to the house for paper and a pencil."

Blake raised an eyebrow. "You're going to interview *Mom*?"

"Yeah."

He was quiet for a moment. "Why don't you just record her? You could use my phone."

"Really?"

He pulled his phone out of his back pocket and typed in the pass code before turning it toward me. "See this microphone icon? It's an app for recording voice memos."

"I know. Mom has the same phone, and she's always recording work stuff she doesn't want to forget."

Blake tapped the phone. "Come to think of it, this thing has video, too."

Video.

Why hadn't I thought of that? I could *film* Mom answering my questions. I didn't have much experience with making videos, and filming with Julian's super-complicated camera had been pretty intimidating. But Blake's phone was lightweight and simple enough for a toddler to operate.

After I filmed the interview, maybe I could get my own shots of Hilliard House, the river, and the cemetery. Mine wouldn't be as good as Julian's—not even close—but at least I'd have control over the story. I'd have a clear purpose, too. My footage would be used for a mystery instead of a horror story. And this was a mystery I could solve . . . but only with Blake's help.

"Hey, what if I use your phone to film Mom when I ask my questions? That would be quicker, right? And then maybe I could film Hilliard House and all the places linked to the mystery of Margaret Anne and Joshua Hilliard. Wouldn't that be cool?"

"So you're going to make your own movie now?"

"Well . . . I'd like to try."

"Maybe I don't trust you with my phone," he said warily. "What if I miss a text?"

"From who? Yourself? There's no signal up here, remember?"

"Still . . ."

"Oh, forget it, then."

I drew my knees to my chest and imagined the copper beech tree eating Blake alive. In my head I could hear the satisfying crunch of his bones, but in real life the silence stretched on for a while.

"Avery?" he finally said. "I should be the one filming since it's my phone."

I stared at him. "You're going to help me?"

"Only to make sure you don't break my phone. When Mom got it for me, she said it would cost hundreds of dollars to replace."

Inside I was smiling, but I made sure to keep my face serious to keep up the game.

"Fine," I said. "You can work the camera, but I don't want you taking over my story. We have to *discuss* things and agree with each other."

He narrowed his eyes. "Discussing things and agreeing with each other means you have to actually listen to me and not go into meltdown if I have a different idea."

"Yeah, yeah. I get it." I grinned. "This could work, Blake. Let's go find Mom."

CHAPTER 24

We found her still sitting under the oak tree, her glass empty and her lap full of Weasley.

"I meant to get up fifteen minutes ago," she said, slowly trailing her fingers along the cat's spine. "But I just don't have the heart to push him off."

"That's easy enough to fix." I scooped Weasley into my arms and set him on the ground. He raised his tail and sauntered away, making sure we had a clear view of his backside.

Mom picked at the fur on her shorts. "What's up, Avery?"

"Remember when we were doing the dishes and I asked you about Joshua Hilliard? Is it okay if I ask you a few more questions about him?"

Her eyes moved to Blake before settling back on me. "Sure, honey."

"Great. Now . . . would it be okay if Blake filmed your answers with his phone?"

"Are you deposing me, Avery?" Her brow wrinkled. "What's this about?"

I tightened my ponytail to stall for a second. When explaining something to Mom, it was important to set things out straight and clear. "You know how Julian and I were making a movie, right? But it turned out bad because he tricked me."

She started to say something but then closed her mouth and nodded slowly.

"Well, I still want to make a movie, sort of like the history I told you we were making, but now it's become more of a *mystery* than a history of Hilliard House. I want to get the facts straight, and that's why I need to ask you some questions."

"That sure was a mouthful."

"Yeah, sorry," I muttered.

She smiled. "So you're turning Ken Burns on me? At the tender age of twelve?"

"Huh?"

"Never mind," she said. "I'm glad to help. Do you want to do this inside?"

"No. The light's good out here, and I want the trees behind the house as a backdrop."

I hustled Mom to her feet and stuck a chair under each arm. Once I had her settled in the chair on the opposite side of the house with the soft afternoon light warming her face, I placed the other chair at a diagonal from her and sat down.

"Okay, Blake, when I give you the signal, start filming. But keep me out of the frame. We'll probably edit out my questions later."

"How?"

"We'll figure it out. I just want the shot to be Mom from the waist up with the trees behind her. Tilt the phone so the picture is wide instead of tall. And make sure her face is in the center of the frame."

Blake grinned. "You got it, boss."

I faced Mom. "Okay, I'm going to ask you a couple of questions, and I just want you to answer with all the things you can remember, only make it sound good and smooth and all. Like on TV."

"That's it, huh?" She straightened up and smoothed her hair.

I turned to Blake. "Ready?"

He nodded.

My heartbeat skittered into a trot. "Okay, start filming." I took a breath. "Mom, I want you to tell us about Joshua Hilliard. Start with how Grandma and Grandpa, and, you know, the folks in the community, saw him. Then tell us how you saw him differently. Because you did see him differently, didn't you?"

She nodded and stared into the distance for a moment. Mom had always told Blake and me to think before speaking, and nobody was better at that than her. When she opened her mouth, she spoke in a cool, calm way.

"By the time I met Joshua Hilliard, he was in his eighties and living on his own in that big, lonely house. He didn't go to church or socialize with the family—that much is true. He kept to himself, and people thought he was strange. My father said he was a good-for-nothing atheist who lost his child through neglect, and who later drove his wife to an early grave."

I couldn't help a little shiver at that.

"But the man I talked to was kind and gentle," she continued. "Terribly sad, though. He told me he left the church because it didn't make sense to him anymore—not after what he'd seen in France during the war. It wasn't that he didn't believe in God. He just longed for peace and forgiveness, and Dad's faith was too much about fear and judgment."

"What about Margaret Anne?" I asked.

"Oh, he adored her. She meant the world to him." Her eyes held mine. "You'll understand when you have kids of your own." She turned back to the camera. "For all he suffered in the war, I think her death was a much greater tragedy. One he could never quite get over."

"How did she die?"

"It did have to do with the floods, but not a drowning, like your friend Julian thought. Mr. Hilliard told me she contracted typhoid from contaminated water, which happened a lot back then when it flooded. His wife had been visiting family on the other side of the river and couldn't get back right away because the water was too high and the ferry wasn't running. By the time she got back, Margaret Anne was on her deathbed. Mr. Hilliard told me his wife blamed him."

"Why?"

"She said he hadn't boiled the water properly, hadn't watched Margaret Anne closely enough, hadn't called the doctor soon enough. Basically, he got everything wrong." Mom shook her head. "I'm sure it was just her grief, but she made her feelings known to everyone in town. She stayed with him a year after Margaret Anne was buried, but then moved back with her folks. The poor man lived alone with the blame for the rest of his life."

"That's pretty tragic," I whispered.

Mom wiped her right eye. "Does that answer all your questions?"

"Yeah . . . I guess that's a cut, Blake."

"Man." Blake lowered the phone. "This mystery of Hilliard House is already starting to bum me out."

"But it feels like I'm finally getting somewhere," I said. "Like we might actually be getting close to something *true.*"

That night after supper I asked Grandma for a higher-watt bulb for my bedside lamp, and I had my speech all prepared.

"Blake and I are working on a project together, and I need to do some planning tonight. It would help to have a brighter light. So I don't permanently damage my eyesight or anything."

Grandma clucked her tongue. "No need to be dramatic, Avery May. Can't you just work at the kitchen table? The light is very bright in there."

"Grandma, I need to work in private, where it's quiet, so I can concentrate." I'd also be staying up late, but I didn't tell her that.

She studied me for a moment, and I just studied her right back without blinking.

"Will sixty watts do?" she finally asked.

Once I'd changed the bulb, I reached down to pull several sheets of drawing paper from the Kingdom box. Then I grabbed the colored pencils and made myself comfortable on the quilt.

Did I know what I was doing? Not really. I couldn't imagine what this movie with Blake would look like when it was finished. I just needed a plan for the next day. Otherwise, he and I would waste too much time arguing.

Weasley watched from the edge of the bed as I divided my

first sheet of paper into eight squares, each one representing an individual shot. When Julian first told me about shots and angles, he'd called this kind of thing a storyboard. With a regular pencil I sketched out how each shot would look. It wasn't the best drawing I could do—just outlines and stick figures so I had an idea of what should go where within the frame.

The opening scene would be a wide shot of the cemetery, panning from left to right to get a sense of the trees that surrounded it, and coming to a stop on me standing next to the Clearview Cemetery sign. I knew from studying those films with Julian that I couldn't just stand there talking for a long time. He would have called that a *static* shot because not enough was happening and the audience would get bored. Maybe it'd be better if I walked toward Joshua Hilliard's grave? I wrote some introductory words in the space left over. That way I could practice it a little before we actually shot the scene.

The next shot had to be the gravestone of Elizabeth and Margaret Anne Hilliard. A close-up first, but then pulling back to include me. This was where I would introduce the story question—why was Joshua Hilliard buried separately from his wife and daughter? Did it have something to do with his daughter's tragic early death?

After that I made a list of short clips we could use to break up long scenes. I had no clue how to edit them in, but Blake and I could figure that out later. I listed all the close-up shots I could think of: the lettering on headstones, drooping grave flowers, carvings, photographs. Maybe even an angel statue.

Weasley attempted several stealth landings on my stack

of papers—he just couldn't resist the crinkle of paper under his paws—so eventually I had to shut him out of the attic. I worked until nearly midnight and only stopped because my eyes were dry and gritty. When I finally turned out the light, I slept hard. Too hard for any dreams to creep in.

CHAPTER 25

"Zoom in on that carving of the cross."

Blake looked up from the headstone. "Avery, there's no zoom on this phone."

"Can't you do that two-finger thing?"

"I tried, but the picture goes out of focus."

"Well, just walk closer to it while the camera's rolling, I guess."

"That's what I've *been* doing."

A bead of sweat plopped into my right eye, so I backed away to rub at it. Something moved in the distance, but when I focused both eyes in that direction, everything was still. Just trees and graves.

My stomach gave a hideous growl.

"Tell me about it," muttered Blake.

It was all taking a lot longer than I'd planned. Even though I'd scripted out what to say, we'd needed eleven takes to get the intro segment even close to right, and fifteen to get the bit by Margaret Anne's grave. I knew this because Blake had numbered each take, his voice growing snarkier each time. On the last take, he'd muttered, "Action. Take *one billion*."

Honestly, I wouldn't have minded Julian stepping in at

that point. He was selfish and took advantage of people, but he knew what he wanted and got the job done. If we didn't finish this day's filming soon, Blake would mutiny on me, and then I'd be up a creek with no cameraman.

"Did you see that?"

I shaded my eyes to look where Blake was pointing but didn't see anything out of the ordinary. "What?"

"I could have sworn I saw somebody."

"This heat could make a person hallucinate." I wiped my forehead on my sleeve. "Look, we just need some shots of grave flowers, the more droopy and tattered, the better, and then we can go back for lunch."

Most of the flowers were fake—silk carnations and roses on knobby plastic stems—but we did find a grave with a built-in vase full of lilies with browning, crinkled edges. I knew from listening to Julian that the contrast of the white petals against the dark gray stone would look even better in black and white. I just had to somehow figure out how to make that change later.

Deeper into the cemetery Blake found a grave with a vase of freshly picked daisies tipped over on its side. Without me even asking he took some footage of the fallen vase, so I stood back and studied the gravestone. It was very similar to Grandpa's—a man's name with birth and death dates at the left, and his wife's name at the right with the death date still blank. It made my heart ache a little to think of old Aileen Forney Shelton bringing fresh wildflowers every week to her husband Clarence only to have the wind blow them over.

Wait . . . *Aileen?*

Her birthday was June 8, 1930.

I ran back to Margaret Anne's grave to check. She was born in 1930, just as I'd thought. My face flushed hot and tingly, and this time it wasn't the sun's fault.

"Are we done with this one?" Blake called.

I walked toward him and set the daisy vase upright again. Then I pointed at the gravestone. "This woman—I'm almost positive she was Margaret Anne's friend. We found a framed photo of Margaret Anne with another girl, and the names written on the back were Margaret Anne and Aileen."

"How do you know it's the same Aileen?"

"Same birth year. And how many Aileens have you seen in the cemetery? It's not an everyday sort of name." I took a breath to calm my thumping heart. "We have to talk to her. We could even get her on camera. Someone who knew Margaret Anne? That would make this film into something *real*. Well, it's real now, but it would be so much cooler."

"You know, Avery, she's probably dead."

"Nice one, brainiac. If she were dead, she'd be *here*. With a death date on her grave."

"Right. Duh." Blake looked away. "But still, she's over eighty years old. She may have lost her mind already." He shivered. "Old people . . . they weird me out."

"Grandma's old and you like her just fine."

"She's different. She's not *that* old, and she's only a little batty."

"Well, this lady brings fresh flowers to her husband's grave, so she must be pretty neat." I imagined a lady knitting in a rocking chair, her soft white hair in a bun and a lace collar around her neck. She'd look so *quaint* on camera. And that was just the sort of thing this film needed.

By the time we got back to the house, Grandma had already settled into her afternoon nap, so Mom made us grilled cheese sandwiches with apples and brown sugar toasted inside.

"How'd your meeting go?" I asked between chews.

"Try swallowing before you speak," Mom said. "The closing is set for three weeks from tomorrow, pending the outcome of the inspection. Mama settled on a lower price in lieu of making repairs, so unless there's something horribly wrong that the buyers didn't find, I think everything will work out fine."

A sliver of apple stuck in my throat. In all the craziness of the past couple of days, I'd forgotten about the Hilliard House inspection. The whole point of such a thing was to look for damage. Had Julian left water in the tub upstairs? There could be water on the floor, too.

"How was your filming at the cemetery?" Mom smiled and shook her head. "Now that's a question I never expected to ask my children."

I looked at Blake.

He shrugged.

"Actually, we found something interesting." I pointed at the folder I'd set on the china cabinet. "Can you hand me that?"

Mom reached for the red folder and set it next to me. I wiped my hands and pulled the photograph of Margaret Anne and Aileen out of the left pocket.

When I held it out to her, she stared at the photo for a moment, her mouth dropping open. "I remember this," she said, wiping her hands before taking it. "Mr. Hilliard showed it to me. But I think it was in a silver frame back then."

"Turn it over, Mom. The other girl is named Aileen, which is a spelling I'd never seen before. At least not until today at the cemetery when I saw the name—spelled exactly the same way—on a gravestone. It was for a man and his wife, but the wife hasn't died yet. Her name is Aileen Forney Shelton, and she was born in 1930, just like Margaret Anne. There's someone alive who knew her!"

"My goodness," Mom said. "The name sounds familiar—I probably met her at one of the cemetery gatherings."

"Do you think she'd be part of our film? That she might talk to us about Margaret Anne?"

Mom took a sip of tea and carefully set the glass down. "Avery, you realize it's been over seventy-five years since Margaret Anne died? Think of all that's happened to Mrs. Shelton in the meantime. She may not remember very much."

"But Grandma always says she remembers things from her childhood better than what she did yesterday. We have to try, don't we?"

Mom smiled. "I suppose we could give her a call."

I sank in my chair. "If we just had Internet on this hill we could do a search on her and maybe find her email address or something."

"If we had Internet," Blake said, "we could use satellites to find the exact location of her house."

"I have an even better idea." Mom stood up, taking her plate to the sink, and walked out of the kitchen. She returned with a skinny yellow book in her hand. "Here's some technology that'll blow your mind. How about we look her up in the phone book?"

I raised an eyebrow at Blake.

Mom sat and paged through the book. "Okay, here's Sheerin, Shehan, Shelsey . . . well, there's no Aileen, but here's a Mrs. Clarence Shelton."

"That's it! Her husband was named Clarence."

"Get a pen and write this number down, Avery."

"And then you'll call her?" I asked.

"Not a chance, my girl."

I gulped.

"This is your project," Mom said. "You make the call."

CHAPTER 26

It took me a while to work up the nerve. Calling someone on the phone was something people did on TV reruns. I kept Mom's old flip phone in my pocket during the school year, but that was only so she and I could reach each other in an emergency. It didn't have a texting plan, and since I kept up with my friends online I never called anyone else on it.

I was so jittery that I ended up writing a script for the conversation, and I asked Mom to look it over.

"I'm not sure why you're so nervous about this," she said.

"I never talk to old people except for Grandma. And talking on the phone is just . . . *stressful*."

Mom's eyes got that faraway look. "My friends and I used to talk for hours on the phone after school. Daddy would get so annoyed. 'Can't you get all that out of your system at school?' But we *never* ran out of things to talk about. And when a boy would call? Sometimes I'd be up past midnight talking on the phone, but I had to be secret about it."

"Okay, Mom. Enough about the golden olden days." I glanced over my script again. "I have to do this in private."

She smiled. "Why don't you use the phone in the sewing

room? That way you can close the door. I'll be in the kitchen if you need me."

Once I'd shut the door and settled in the rolling chair, I punched in the numbers. The phone rang and rang. Just when I was about to hang up, it finally connected and a rough voice said, "Hello?"

"Um, hello. Is this Mrs. Shelton?"

"No, it isn't."

"Could I speak with Mrs. Shelton, please?"

There was a pause. "Who is this?"

It took my last ounce of courage not to hang up. "This is Avery May Hilliard. My grandma is Ava Hilliard."

"Miss Ava, huh? Church of Christ?"

"Yes, ma'am."

"Why do you need to speak with my aunt?"

I glanced at my script, which had been written as if I was talking to Mrs. Shelton, not some niece who didn't even give her name. "Well, um, I was hoping to talk to Mrs. Shelton about . . . what I mean is, I'm doing a project on local history, and I need to talk to some old folks." I cringed. "Er, I need people who have been in the area for a while and know the history. People who knew my family. I think your aunt was friends with one of my relatives when they were little girls."

The woman sighed. "Aunt Aileen doesn't talk on the phone much. She doesn't do much of anything anymore, because she tires easily."

"But I really need to ask her some questions. I'll do whatever it takes."

She didn't answer, and the silence dragged on for at least a century.

"Are you still there, ma'am?"

"You'd have to come here," she finally said. "How old are you, anyway?"

"I'm twelve. But I promise I'm serious about this project, ma'am. I can get my mom to bring me, and I won't be loud or track in dirt or anything."

There was another awkward pause before she spoke.

"You could come by tomorrow morning. She's at her best before noon. I suppose any time between nine and eleven would work. It's not like she has anywhere to go or any other appointments to keep."

Relief made my knees wobbly. "That sounds great. I'll just check with my mom."

"You be sure to call if you can't make it. I don't want to waste time getting her ready for a no-show."

"I promise I'll be there. Thank you."

After I'd put the phone back on the charger, I went to the kitchen. Mom had her computer open on the kitchen table, and she looked up when I stood next to her.

"Everything all right?" she asked.

"Mrs. Shelton's niece answered the phone. She sounded a little cranky, but she told me to come tomorrow morning. You'll drive me, right?"

"I'd be happy to. Well done, honey."

I lay my cheek on her head. "There's one thing. What exactly is typhoid? I probably should know, since that's how Margaret Anne died."

"Well . . . it's an infection, I think. You get it from contaminated food or water." She started to type, but then shook her head. "I can't check the Internet, so if you want to know more, you'll have to look it up in Grandma's *World Book Encyclopedia*. She got that set in the eighties, but it's not like typhoid has changed that much in the last thirty years."

I went to the living room and pulled the *T* volume off the shelf. The pages were thick and shiny with a sickly sweet smell that made my nose twitch. The entry for "typhoid" was long and I had to read it a few times before I got the gist. Turns out that typhoid is a bacterial disease you get from eating food or drinking water that has feces in it.

Feces? How in the world did anyone manage to eat or drink something with *poo* in it?

Actually, there were *lots* of ways. One way was not to wash your hands after going to the bathroom. Flies feeding on poo was another—if those flies landed on your food they could give you the disease. Or if your water supply got mixed up with sewage, the water could get contaminated. Back in Margaret Anne's day, the water wasn't even chlorinated, so there was a bigger risk. Mom had said that flooding could help spread typhoid. It made me gag a little to think about it, but I could see how sewage and drinking water might get mixed up if water was overflowing everywhere.

The symptoms of typhoid were high fever, stomach pain, headache, and tiredness. Sometimes the bacteria could get to your intestines and then leak into your abdominal cavity, and that could lead to death.

No wonder Joshua Hilliard had been maudlin. It must have been torture to watch his little girl suffer like that. And since his wife was out of town, he was the only one around to take care of Margaret Anne. But why didn't he call the doctor before it was too late? Did the flooding have something to do with it?

Maybe Aileen Shelton would know.

CHAPTER 27

"This is it," Mom said.

I leaned toward the window and saw SHELTON stenciled on the mailbox when she turned off the main road. The tires kicked up gravel as we crept along the driveway toward a little white house with green shutters and a front porch. The siding was dusty and the gutter sagged a little, but Grandma would have called the house "respectable enough."

I got out of the car and gathered my notebook to my chest for comfort. Blake messed with his hair, pushing it forward in that way that nearly covered his eyes. Mom waited by the front of the car.

We all stared at one another for a moment.

"Go on, Mom," I said. "We'll follow."

She shook her head. "*You* need to ring the doorbell, Avery."

It was no use giving her the pitiful look, so I dragged myself up the porch steps and took a deep breath. The doorbell was cracked, but I heard it chime from inside when I pressed it. After a moment, the door opened to reveal a dark-haired lady with half an inch of gray roots and no makeup. She wore a blue velour tracksuit and didn't look old enough to be Mrs. Shelton.

"You must be Avery May." She peered closer. "You've got your grandma's pointy chin, all right."

Her face drooped in a frown, and she smelled like cigarettes.

"Are you gonna come in or what?" the woman said. "Aunt Aileen is in her bedroom. You did know she's bedridden, didn't you?"

My shoulders tensed up. "I've never interviewed anyone from their bed before."

"You just have to pull up a chair. For some reason she's eager to see you." She looked past me. "Who'd you bring with you?"

"Just my mom and brother."

The woman shrugged. "Well, all of y'all had better come in."

She led us toward the back of the house to a flowery-walled room with lots of light coming in through the windows. A small lady lay in the bed with quilts pulled up to her chest. She wasn't propped up very much, and I wondered if she was even able to sit upright anymore. Her cheeks were wrinkled and kind of sunken, and you could see the pink of her scalp through thinning white hair.

One of her veiny hands beckoned. "Is that you, Avery May? I know I'm a sight, but don't be afraid. I'm just old, is all. People don't visit me much anymore, especially not charming young ladies."

I straightened up and smiled, happy to take it as a compliment, even if it was just her old-fashioned manners.

Mrs. Shelton pointed a knobby finger. "See that chair? Pull it up next to me and I'll tell you all I know about the history around here. And who did you bring with you? I can barely see anymore."

"Oh, sorry. This is my mom, Maddie Hilliard, and behind her is my brother, Blake."

"I'm not sure there's enough room in here for everyone." She raised her chin and bellowed. "Loretta, why don't you get Avery May's mother a glass of Coke in the parlor? The young gentleman might want one, too."

"Actually," I said quickly, "I was hoping he could stay and film our conversation. It's for the documentary I'm making."

Mrs. Shelton's eyes widened. "Mercy! Are you telling me that handsome young man brought a camera for filming? Does he need space to set everything up?"

"He uses his smartphone." I glanced at Blake, who was looking kind of squirmy. "It makes pretty decent videos."

"The good Lord knows I'm old, but you two are making me feel like Methuselah."

"Would you rather not be filmed, Mrs. Shelton?" asked Mom.

"No, no, it's fine. It's something new, and I thought I'd seen it all. Loretta, is my hair looking all right?"

"Your hair is as good as it gets, Aunt Aileen. Do you have any lipstick or powder around here?"

"Lord, no. I'm past all that." She turned to me and patted my arm. "Honey, will you just tell me if I start drooling?"

Ordinarily that would have grossed me out, but her cozy way of talking made me feel at home. "No problem, Mrs. Shelton."

"All right, then. Loretta, you be sure to open a fresh bottle of Coke. The real stuff, not that Kroger brand."

Loretta sighed. "Yes, ma'am."

Mrs. Shelton nodded and turned back to me. "Well, Miss Avery May Hilliard, are you ready to get to work?"

I took a seat and waited for Mom and Loretta to move on to the parlor. Then I checked my notes and gave Blake the thumbs-up to start filming.

"I was hoping you could help me with some family history. I found this in the old Hilliard House." I pulled the photo out of the notebook's inside pocket. "It's a photograph, and I think you're in it."

Mrs. Shelton took the photo and peered at it. Then she snorted. "Sweetheart, would you hand me that magnifying glass on the side table? Yes, that's it. Without it all I can see are two blobs." She propped the photo on her belly with one hand and held the magnifier in the other. The glass shook a little as she stared at the photo.

"That's me, all right. I sure was a scrawny thing back then. Guess some things never change." She started to laugh, but it ended in a wet cough. "That's Margaret Anne Hilliard next to me. She was your grandpa's cousin." She nodded to herself. "All those golden curls always falling out of ribbons. Her hair had a mind of its own, I tell you."

"What was Margaret Anne like? Were you good friends?"

"Good friends? It was more than that." Her eyes softened. "We were nothing alike, but we were kindred spirits. I called her Meganne, because her real name had too many syllables. Her mama hated the nickname, though—she thought it 'common'—so I only called her that when we were alone."

"Meganne," I said. "I like that."

Mrs. Shelton nodded. "Her mother's folks owned the

land we farmed, so whenever Meganne visited her grandma, we would spend as much time together as possible. She was a dreamy gal, loved stories and such. Me? I was a girl of action. I suppose she taught me to be a little more thoughtful, and I taught her how to be brave, how to take risks and live life."

She settled back with a smile, as if thinking about Meganne made her feel young again.

"We found something else at Hilliard House, Mrs. Shelton," I said. "An old china doll with gold hair and a pink dress. Did that belong to Meganne?"

"Her name is Bettina." She grinned. "Can you believe that sprang to my mind so quick? Bettina was a gift from Meganne's daddy. She came all the way from Germany and was quite a treasure. More than anything, she was a comfort when that poor girl was confined to her bed, which was often. I was forever trying to get Meganne to take long walks, to breathe fresh air, because she needed strengthening up. I was half her size but strong as a bull. She tended to get every little bug that came along."

"Is that why she got typhoid?"

Mrs. Shelton winced. "That was . . . well, that was a real tragedy."

I straightened and took a breath. "How'd it happen? Was it the flood?"

She closed her eyes, and the photograph trembled in her hands. "I couldn't say for sure. By the time her daddy got hold of the doctor, there wasn't much that could be done."

A bead of sweat trickled near my eye. I glanced at Blake, whose armpits now had dark circles of perspiration. The room had seemed warm when we came in, but now it was practically boiling. I waited for Mrs. Shelton to continue, but the silence stretched on.

"Did she drink contaminated water, Mrs. Shelton?" I finally prompted.

She swallowed hard before opening her eyes. The next words were spoken to the ceiling. "Everyone said that Mr. Hilliard didn't take the proper precautions. That's what his wife claimed, anyway, and her story got around real quick."

"It makes me sad for old Mr. Hilliard," I said. "He told my mom he did everything he could, but people blamed him anyway. Grandma says he turned maudlin and shut himself up in his house. Did you ever see him again after Margaret Anne died?"

"Once or twice, I suppose." Mrs. Shelton closed her eyes again.

"Did he seem strange to you? Did he talk to you about her?"

"It's so hard to remember, child."

"But—"

Blake put a hand on my shoulder, and I shut my mouth.

A tear trailed down the side of Mrs. Shelton's face. She handed the photo back to me without opening her eyes.

"Young lady, I'm afraid you've worn me out," she said.

My heart lurched. I wasn't ready for this to end—she'd barely told me anything.

"I only have a couple more questions, ma'am."

"I've said all I have to say." Mrs. Shelton pulled a tissue from her sleeve and dabbed at her eyes. "It's time for you to leave."

CHAPTER 28

We drove home in silence. Mom was sure I'd said something to offend Mrs. Shelton, and nothing Blake or I could say would convince her otherwise. So after a gloomy lunch of cold sandwiches and Mom's even colder stare, I escaped to the attic. I had to push that poor old lady out of my mind somehow, and storyboarding the final shots at Hilliard House seemed the best option. These shots would be the last we filmed, but in the sequence of the movie, they would come right after the opening cemetery scene.

Once again I divided several sheets of paper into eight blocks. The establishing shot would be the house, shot from a low angle so it looked proud and spooky. Then maybe Blake could pull back, and I would enter the frame and talk about the history of the house. Like how a smaller house with wood siding stood there first, but when it burned down, this fancy brick house was built to take its place. I'd talk about Joshua Hilliard's service in the Great War, and how he married a pretty young lady soon after. And then I'd talk about Margaret Anne.

Just like in the cemetery, we'd have to get close-up shots of the house and interesting details here and there that could be edited in to break up the long scenes of me talking. I made a list of possible shots, trying to think like Julian. He would pay special attention to peeling paint on woodwork, to crumbling brick and concrete, or maybe even to a browned-out patch of grass. We could do some wide shots of the river, too, and the land surrounding the house. I hoped more ideas would come to me once we got there.

The door at the foot of the stairs creaked open.

"Avery, can I come up?"

"Yeah, Mom."

I gathered the different storyboard pages, but didn't have time to put them back in the box. Weasley appeared first and jumped on the pile of pages, purring as the paper crackled under his feet.

Mom paused at the top of the stairs. "You doing okay?"

"Mom, I *promise* I didn't say anything rude to Mrs. Shelton. She was chatting away about Margaret Anne, happy as could be. She wasn't the least bit choked up to talk about her. But when I started asking about Mr. Hilliard, she clammed right up. And I'm not sure why, because she wouldn't say anything more about it. She just started crying and asked us to leave."

Mom sat on the bed next to me. "I may have overreacted, but I hate the thought of you bullying that poor old woman with your questions."

"I've never bullied anyone!"

She gave me a sideways glance. "Oh, really? You can be pretty forceful sometimes. I just assumed you'd go easy on a delicate, bedridden lady."

"I did go easy. Ask Blake. You and Grandma taught me to be polite to old folks."

"To your *elders*," Mom corrected with a half smile. "Will the interview still work for your film?"

"I guess. We got a few new details, but I thought she'd have a lot more to tell me."

"Like I said before, she was very young when she knew Margaret Anne, and so many years have passed." She pointed at the storyboards. "You about ready to finish this project?"

"Yeah." I gently pushed Weasley off the pages and smoothed them in my lap. "I'd just hoped for something bigger. Julian told me an artist has to take risks, and I took plenty. Seems like I should have learned more."

Mom leaned in and kissed my cheek. She smelled like Grandma's Dove soap rather than her usual perfume, and it was so soft and sweet that I kind of sank into her.

"I can't say I'm happy with all your actions since you got here, but I am proud of you for taking on this project," she said. "You've grown up a lot this summer."

"Enough that you won't keep secrets from me anymore?"

She drew back to look me in the eye. "Is the father issue still bothering you?"

I turned away, expecting that sick feeling in my gut. But it didn't come. "Not as much, I guess."

"Avery, if you ever have a question about me, I'll answer it as honestly as I can. I won't know what's bugging you unless you tell me." She smoothed a piece of hair out of my eyes and tucked it behind my ear.

I still couldn't look at her. "I've been telling people my dad is dead. It was . . . easier."

Mom put her hand on my cheek and turned my face toward her. "I want you to think about secrets and honesty, and not just regarding your father. There's a lot that you've been keeping from Grandma, too."

"Yeah, because I don't want to die."

She smiled. "I'm going to pack. Will you keep Weasley up here so he doesn't jump in my suitcase? And, Avery, let's all make a special effort to get along during supper. I want to leave on a high note."

Mom had an early flight the next morning because she had a hearing scheduled for Monday and needed the weekend to prepare. She never seemed to get enough time off, but we were pretty used to it by now. One time when she was really tired and crabby, she told us that making partner in a law firm was like winning a pie-eating contest where the prize for eating the most pie was . . . more pie. Only she used a bad word instead of "pie."

The four of us ate breakfast together at the airport café. Mom and Grandma behaved themselves all morning, but even I could see the relief on Mom's face when she waved at us before joining the security line.

The clouds were low and dark on the drive back, but only a few fat drops came down. By the time we got to the house, the air was so thick you could practically swim in it.

"The garden will sit for a day," Grandma said as she pulled into the carport. "You two should make yourself some sandwiches . . . and then you might do a rain dance for a proper downpour. Actually, I don't mind what you do as long as you stay out of my hair until supper."

Grandma was always grumpy after taking Mom to the airport, so it was a good thing Blake and I already had a plan for the afternoon. We packed a lunch of sandwiches and homemade brownies and headed out the door.

When we passed through the thicket of trees and Hilliard House loomed ahead, I turned to Blake. "Can you get footage of this view? It looks cool with the gloomy sky behind it."

He took some video. Then he took a few photos and showed me one with different filters. The black-and-white version, with its edges kind of blackened and torn, gave me a little shiver.

"Does it bother you to be here again?" he asked.

I stared at the house. "Julian and Lily made all that stuff up. I don't think the house bothered me until I got in trouble with Grandma when I was little, and then all I could think of was the whipping she gave me. And when I told Julian about that, he did his best to make the house seem scary. But it was all lies, right?"

Blake nodded slowly.

A blob of sweat trickled down the side of my face. "Let's sit under that tree and eat first," I said. "I need to cool down before we start filming."

Blake studied the storyboards while we ate. "We could start with a shot of you sitting on the porch step," he said. "And after you do your introduction, I could pull back to reveal the whole building—that would be cool, don't you think?"

I considered it. "Yeah, that might work."

"And I like that rusty old water pump over there. It would make a good shot to show the character of the place." He took a bite of sandwich and kept on talking. "I mean, added to the ones you wrote down."

"You're actually getting into this filmmaking stuff, aren't you?"

He swallowed hard. "Excuse me?"

"I thought you were just doing it because you felt sorry for me or something. Or maybe Mom put you up to it."

"Does that even sound like me?"

"Well, you didn't want to do Kingdom with me, so . . ."

He groaned. "I don't know why you took that so personally. I just . . . Kingdom didn't work for me anymore. It was getting a little lame, you know, with the pretending and everything."

"But we're still telling a story."

"There's more action to this filmmaking stuff. It's *hands on*." He took another bite and then talked with his mouth full. "Can we please not analyze it to death?"

After we'd packed up the trash, I sat on the front step and practiced my lines while Blake did his close-up shots. By the time we got around to filming, I only needed two takes to get it right.

"Turns out I'm pretty awesome at this," I said after we'd watched the clips.

"Yeah, but the learning curve was steep." He swiped through the previous clips. "You want to watch all the bad takes we had at the cemetery? There's only about five thousand of them."

I grabbed at the phone. "Just delete that stuff, Blake."

"No way!" He clutched the phone to his chest and grinned. "I'm saving them for the gag reel on the DVD release."

I couldn't help a little giggle at that, but when his expression changed I hushed right up. Blake had shifted his gaze to something behind me, and whatever he saw made him frown.

"What the heck?" he muttered.

I turned around in time to see a familiar figure ducking behind a cedar tree.

CHAPTER 29

"We saw you, Julian!" I shouted. "Might as well come out."

After a moment he did. He was wearing his backpack, and that camera was hanging from his neck as usual. His shoulders were kind of slumped, though, and it looked like he'd been picking at the scab on his cheek.

"So you're the infamous Julian Wayne." Blake crossed his arms. "You better be here to apologize. Otherwise, you're trespassing." He turned to me. "You want me to take care of this?"

I have to admit it was nice to have my brother acting all chivalrous, like a knight from Kingdom. And I was supposed to still be mad at Julian—I *knew* that—but somehow I couldn't help feeling kind of relieved to see him.

"It's okay," I said. "What do you want, Julian?"

"I just, um, wanted to talk to you," he said quietly.

"Was that you at the cemetery? You could have said hi instead of hiding behind trees like a creeper."

Julian sighed. "You were still mad, Avery. And it looked like you were making your own movie, so I figured you wouldn't want to talk to me."

"But you're still following us," Blake said. "What's your deal?"

Julian turned to face the house. "I keep thinking about that place. I've even tried to get inside again."

"But you gave the key back."

He turned to me. "The day after you got scared and everything—"

"The day after you *tricked* me," I interrupted.

He nodded slowly. "That day, I went to town with Dad and made a copy of the key . . . because it wasn't over."

"Man," said Blake, "you really are a shifty little punk."

Julian met his gaze. "I didn't mean to be shifty. I just get so . . . *caught up* in my movie projects."

"You can't go in Hilliard House whenever you want," I said.

"I went about this all wrong—I *know* that—but there's something going on in that house." His hand went to the scab on his cheek. "You think you're done with it, but I'm not sure the house is done with us."

Blake snorted. "What does that even mean? Avery said you made all that stuff up."

"It's hard to explain," Julian said. "But I can show you."

Blake looked at me, eyebrows raised. I glanced at Julian and saw how hard his eyes were pleading. I'd been pretty mad at him, and for good reason, but I'd also missed how excited he got about filming. I *wanted* to believe him.

"Lead the way, then," I finally said.

Blake and I followed Julian back to the front porch. When we reached the porch steps, Julian gestured for me to go ahead. "I need you to unlock the door."

I frowned. "Why don't you do it?"

"That would be a bad idea." He fiddled with the camera strap. "Probably best that it's not me. Not yet."

I took the steps slowly and studied the front door for a moment. I hadn't felt spooked at all standing on the porch step while Blake filmed me talking about the house, but holding the copied key and working up the nerve to go inside was a different matter.

"This better not be a setup."

"If it is, you're dead meat," Blake said.

"It's not a setup," Julian said evenly. "I can't show you what I'm talking about if you don't open the door."

I put the key in the lock. It turned easily, and I pushed the door open without a problem. At first all I felt was chilly air. Musty like before, but also shivery with damp cold.

"Freaky." Blake rubbed his arms. "I'm getting goose bumps."

"Step inside," Julian said.

I glared at him. "I'm *not* going back upstairs."

"You don't have to. Just take a few steps inside."

With the first step, that familiar queasiness came over me—the wave of heat and cold. But I'd braced myself for this. I knew it was the dark feeling Grandma had felt all those years ago, as if anger and sorrow had twined together and festered for decades.

"I feel it, Julian."

He walked past me toward the staircase. On the bottom step sat the doll, Bettina, but her head had come off and someone had set it on the step above. Looking at that head with its dead eyes staring back at me put a hollow ache in my stomach.

"The head broke off when Lily dropped it," Julian said. "But that's not what I wanted to show you." He placed his hand on the banister and took the first step.

"I'm here," he called out.

I half expected to hear a ghostly voice answer him, but at first there was only silence.

Then I heard a creaking. More than one creaking, actually. I listened hard—the noise was coming from both floors.

"What is that?" I asked.

"It's the doors. They're opening wide all over the house."

"You've got to be kidding," Blake said.

I wrapped my arms around my body. "I think we should go."

"Just wait," Julian said.

"I don't like this," I whispered.

There was a quiet pause. A perfect stillness fell over the house, and all I could hear was the blood rushing in my ears.

Then every door in the house slammed shut.

Blake jerked around to face me, panic in his eyes. "What is going on?"

Before I could answer, the chandelier above us began to sway. The fixture in Margaret Anne's room had done the same thing, but this one was ten times bigger. And all that metalwork with pointy candles and dangling crystals made it so much heavier. Its chain was old, rusted, and the wiring looked frayed.

If that thing fell, it could kill someone.

"We've gotta get out of here." Blake grabbed my arm and steered me toward the door.

I turned back to Julian, but he still hadn't moved from

the staircase. He stared at the fixture and slowly raised his camera.

There was a terrible sound of cracking plaster, and the light fixture pulled away from the ceiling. Pieces of molding broke off and crashed to the floor. The fixture was holding on by the electrical cord, which was shredding from the weight.

Blake pushed me toward the door just as the wire snapped and the entire fixture came crashing to the floor.

CHAPTER 30

I shot through the doorway like a cannonball and took the steps two at a time, only turning when Julian slammed the door on his way out. None of us slowed down until Hilliard House was hidden by the trees. Blake was barely winded, but Julian and I were both doubled over.

"That . . . certainly . . . never happened before," Julian gasped.

Blake stared at Julian through narrowed eyes. "I was sure that chandelier had crashed on your head. You better tell us *exactly* what happened last time you were in the house."

Julian peered up at him. "Can I sit down . . . and catch my breath first?"

"Walk it off. You can talk as we go."

Julian wiped his face on his sleeve, frowning at Blake all the while, and then fell into step beside me. Once he got his breathing under control, he stared straight ahead as he spoke. "The night Avery and I filmed, I felt something shove me against the wall, and my headlamp blew up. I mean, literally—the bulb exploded. And Lily said right before it happened she saw a man's shadow in the mirror."

Blake glanced at me. "But he told her to say stuff like that, right?"

"That wasn't part of the script," Julian said. "We made up the ghost of Margaret Anne—I admit that—but Lily says she saw that shadow in the mirror for real. She's an actress, but she hardly ever improvises. Things got real in that bathroom, and when that happens, Lily doesn't lie."

Blake looked to me again for confirmation.

"He's telling the truth about the shoving and the head-lamp," I said. "I don't know about the rest."

"Anyway . . ." Julian took a deep breath. "When I went back on my own, the doors slammed just like today. The light fixture started swinging, too, but I left pretty quickly. That must have weakened the chain, though."

"Okay," I said. "Maybe Grandma will believe the fixture fell on its own—you know, because it's so old. She could knock a few hundred off the selling price, right?"

"But whoever's buying it would be in danger," Blake said. "Seriously, that house could kill someone."

"Crap." I rubbed my eyes. "Why couldn't you just leave it alone, Julian? You've made everything worse, and now I'm going to be in deep trouble with Grandma."

Julian stopped walking to stare at me. "I made up some stuff, but I didn't create that thing in the house. We just woke it up. Maybe we're doing your grandma a favor."

"But if you'd never tricked me in the first place, it might have stayed asleep!"

"How do you know that? You were the one having cozy chats with it years ago, Avery. *I* didn't start this."

"Don't you dare put this on me." Tears pricked my eyes. "You *twisted* it."

"I just wanted to make a good film. One with *real* emotion. And I really thought it might help you face your fear. But every time I try something like that, I get in trouble." Julian swallowed. "I didn't mean to hurt anyone. Why is everyone so *freaking sensitive*?"

And with that he took off down the hill by himself.

Blake and I stood still for a long moment.

"Well, *now* what do we do?" Blake finally said.

I wiped my forehead on my sleeve. "I don't know . . . run away and join the circus?"

"*I'm* not joining the circus. *I* didn't do anything wrong."

"Then . . . I guess we have to tell Grandma."

"Correction—*you* have to tell her."

I sighed. "Can't you be there, too? I know it's on me to explain everything, but I don't think I can face her alone."

He didn't answer for a long time.

"Blake?"

"As long as you make it clear I had nothing to do with this . . ."

I nodded.

"I guess I can be there when you tell her."

"Thanks." I kind of wanted to hug him, but I knew he'd hate that. Plus he was really sweaty.

"Should we head back?"

I shook my head. "I need to do some research first, and I don't think Grandma's encyclopedias are going to be much help."

"What kind of research?"

"How much battery have you got left on your phone?"

He pulled it from his pocket and swiped the screen with his thumb. "A little less than fifty percent. But it's too slow up here, Avery. We'd go crazy waiting for pages to load."

"We'll have to walk out to the highway, then. We'll walk until you get enough bars or Gs or whatever you need. Grandma's probably taking her nap, so now's as good a time as any, right?"

Turned out we had to walk down the hill, past the cemetery, and all the way to the four-lane highway before Blake could get a decent signal. Once we'd settled ourselves on a grassy patch near the parking lot of Cee Cee's Crafts and Curiosities, I pulled out my storyboard pages and flipped them over to take notes.

Blake looked at me expectantly. "So?"

"Type in *what is a ghost*," I said.

"Don't we kind of know that already?"

"Explain it to me, then, genius."

"Well, when a person dies, sometimes they don't die all the way, and then . . . wasn't there some Bruce Willis movie about this?" He frowned. "All right, I got nothing. Just don't hang over my shoulder while I type."

I readied my pencil.

"It's all obvious stuff," he said after a moment, "like 'an apparition of a dead person,' or 'the energy of a person who has died and is stuck between this plane of existence and the next.'"

I didn't even bother to write that down. "Try *why do ghosts haunt*."

Blake typed in the words with quick, reassuring clicks. "Hold on, it's thinking." After a pause his eyes widened. "Wow, there's a lot of stuff for that. 'Ghosts haunt because they have unfinished business.' That's pretty good. Or how about this: 'Ghosts haunt places or people so they can seek justice for a wrong that happened to them before they died.'"

He read silently for a moment.

"What else?"

"Well, there's totally obvious stuff, like ghosts not knowing they're dead, or ghosts being improperly buried—do you think it's that second one? What if the ghost is Joshua Hilliard, and he's upset that he was buried apart from this wife and child?"

I shook my head. "His wife wanted it that way—that's what Mom told me—and he must have agreed to it since she died long before him."

He turned back to his phone. "Well, how about this: 'Some ghosts return to reenact a crisis from their former lives, most often their death.' That sounds like Margaret Anne. She had a miserable death, didn't she?"

"Yeah, but I don't think she's the ghost."

"Why?"

"Because I'm pretty sure it wasn't Margaret Anne I spoke to when I was in the house. I think it was a grown-up."

He looked up. "Really? You've remembered more?"

"Not exactly. I just know I wasn't afraid when I was in the house back then. The fear of that house came after Grandma whipped me. And when Mom told me she used to visit Mr. Hilliard, and that he was nice to her, it sounded familiar to me."

"You're saying the ghost *is* Joshua Hilliard?"

"It makes a lot more sense than Margaret Anne."

"But wait a minute," Blake said. "If he was a nice old man to Mom, and a nice ghost to you, why would he be so angry now?"

"Type *why do ghosts get angry.*"

He spent a long time scrolling through the results. "There's not a clear answer to that one. But there's a page on the 'psychology of ghosts.' Hold on while I read through this."

He read for so long I couldn't help looking over his shoulder.

"Just give me a second," he said. "Okay, it talks about jealous and fearful ghosts, but I don't think that's our problem. Wait, here's a 'melancholy ghost.'" He read silently again before nodding. "It says, 'someone so overwhelmed by tragedy that they wander the physical realm, unable to move on because they are paralyzed by grief.'"

"That sounds right."

"Listen to this: 'Melancholy ghosts can fill a room with an atmosphere of sadness or despair that profoundly affects the living.'"

"Grandma felt that. So did I, but only after we'd been filming in the house for a while. But do melancholy ghosts get angry?"

"Angry ghosts are their own category." He scrolled some more. "This mostly talks about vengeful ghosts, but listen to this: 'The angry ghost may exhibit poltergeist-like activity, such as hurling objects or physically attacking a person.'"

"Our ghost hasn't really attacked anyone, though."

"What do you call dropping a light fixture on a kid's head?"

"But Julian said he was well out of the way . . ." I frowned. "You're right. Julian was pushed against the wall and his headlamp exploded. You could call that an attack."

"Angry ghost it is." Blake scrolled through the rest of the text. "The only other thing this article says is that you can feed a ghost's anger by sending negative emotions its way. Seems like Julian scaring you on purpose for a ghost movie about Joshua Hilliard's beloved daughter would count for that."

"How do we fix it?"

"I'm going to ask how to get rid of a ghost."

"No! That's too negative. Sounds like an exorcism or something. How about *how do I help a ghost move on*."

Blake read for a long time after that, clicking link after link and shaking his head. "Some of these websites say to bring in a medium. One said we should send love to the spirit and pray to the archangel Michael, and this one says we need to smudge the house with burning sage." He clicked the phone off. "This is all goofy stuff, and I'm running low on battery anyway."

We walked back to the house in silence, but that didn't bother me. I was already rehearsing what I'd say to Grandma. She hated Hilliard House and did not hold with the notion of ghosts, so I would have to explain things in the right order and with lots of evidence, just like my language arts teacher was always rattling on about.

It would've been a lot easier if I had access to Julian's film footage. He must have filmed that swinging light fixture when he was there by himself, and Grandma would *have* to take notice of that. When we passed Hollyhock Cottage, I gave a quick glance at Julian's window, but the curtains were closed. No way was I knocking on the door after his hissy fit.

Then it hit me. What if the Waynes left tomorrow? What if I never talked to Julian again? He'd tricked me, all right, but I'd turned right around and called him *crazy*. I'd said loud and clear—in front of his baby sister—that he should be locked up just like his mother. It had to be the meanest thing I'd ever said to anyone.

"Avery?"

I turned to Blake. "What?"

"Your face is all twisted and intense. What are you thinking?"

I sighed. "Well . . ."

I couldn't tell him about Julian. It was too private, and my words had been too vicious. I didn't want to speak them again, even if it was just to explain what happened.

"I . . . well, I've just been wondering what Joshua Hilliard's 'unfinished business' might be," I finally said. "Or how he might have been wronged when he was alive. Grandma says he wasn't a Christianly man, and that everyone knew Margaret Anne died because of his neglect. But Mom says he was kind and that he would have done everything possible for Margaret Anne, right? And then there's old Aileen Shelton. She clammed up and got all sad when we started talking about Joshua Hilliard and Margaret

Anne's death. I think there's something going on with that."

Blake chewed his lip for a moment. "Sounds plausible."

"So . . . somehow we need to convince Mrs. Shelton to tell us the whole truth. If I can do that, maybe I'll be ready to tell Grandma everything."

CHAPTER 31

Grandma was shuffling around in her room when we got back to the house, so I knew she was just getting up from her afternoon nap. That gave me enough time. I jotted down all the things I needed to say on the pad of paper Grandma kept by the phone in the sewing room. Then I double-checked Aileen Shelton's number and took the phone upstairs.

It rang four times before anyone picked up.

"Hello?" The voice on the other end was faint and raspy.

"Is this Mrs. Shelton? It's Avery May."

"Pardon?"

"Avery May Hilliard. Ava Hilliard's granddaughter."

"Oh."

"Please don't hang up. It's about Hilliard House, Mrs. Shelton. There's something wrong there."

She cleared her throat. "What can you mean, child? No one's lived in that house for decades."

"No one that's actually alive."

There was a pause. "What did you say?"

"Nobody lives there, Mrs. Shelton." I took a breath for courage. "But my brother and I have felt something. *Someone.*"

"I am too old for nonsense, child."

She sure wasn't making this easy on me. I took a deep breath and studied my notes for a second.

"Hello? Are you still there, young lady?"

"Yes, ma'am. I'm trying to tell you there's a presence in the house, and it's not happy. I'm pretty sure it's old Joshua Hilliard."

Silence.

"Mrs. Shelton?"

"I can't decide if this is some piece of mischief you're trying to pull on me."

"No, ma'am. I don't mean any mischief. My grandma would kill me for such a thing."

Mrs. Shelton made a huffing sound.

"I'm calling because . . . well, I think you know a lot more about Joshua Hilliard than you told us. I promise I wouldn't bug you if it wasn't important. I just really need your help."

"What do you expect me to do, child? I'm confined to my bed."

"You don't have to leave your bed, Mrs. Shelton. All I'm asking is for you to tell us the whole story."

Another silence followed, but I just let it be. This was one of Mom's litigator tricks—people hate silence, so if you let it go on long enough, they'll fill it.

Finally Mrs. Shelton groaned. "There's really something in that house?"

"It's already hurt someone, and I'm afraid it could do a lot worse."

She didn't answer right away, and it took all my strength to hold my tongue until she finally spoke.

"You'd better come by tomorrow."

"But—"

"Tomorrow morning," she said. "And bring that photograph of Meganne."

There was a click and the line went dead.

After that I spent some time planning exactly what to tell Grandma. I even made a list of all the possible things she might say or ask and tried to imagine my responses. Yeah, I was procrastinating, but if I'd learned one thing from this summer, it was that planning ahead actually worked. It was kind of the same as Mom telling me to count to five before I blew my top. Just taking a moment to think might help me *not* make an idiot of myself.

Someone pounded on the door. Before I could say anything, it opened, and Blake shouted up the stairs.

"Avery, you'd better come down."

"I know. Just hold on a second."

I put the notes under my pillow and smoothed my ponytail. Even though my heart was thumping, I felt ready. Grandma would be furious, but after I'd explained everything, she'd understand. And she'd know what to do next.

I went downstairs, put the phone back in its charger in the sewing room, and made my way to the living room. The sight of Blake in the old rocking chair eased my mind a little. He'd stuck to his word about not abandoning me. Grandma would be sitting on the sagging couch, and I would take the chair across from her. That was how I'd seen it going down in my head.

But when I turned the corner, someone else was already sitting in that chair with Weasley in his lap.

"Hey, Avery May," said Curtis Wayne. "Julian told me what's been going on."

Sometimes when you read a book and a character gets a big shock, the description says, "All the blood drained from her face." That used to bother me, because I'd always imagined the blood spurting out of the character's pores or something. I'd see it in my mind like a film clip on a continuous loop. It was so distracting that I'd lose interest in the story.

But at that moment my face went so cold that I could feel the blood leaching away, and I knew it was taking the back door to my heart, which had started to pound triple time.

Grandma patted the spot next to her. "Have a seat, Avery May."

She didn't exactly look angry. Her forehead was pretty smooth. But her lips were thin and gray, which told me she was doing her best to keep a tight lid on her anger in the presence of company.

"Mr. Wayne just shared with us how you and Julian have been filming at Hilliard House. Which was very interesting to me, seeing as I'd forbidden you to go inside that house."

Curtis Wayne leaned forward. "I didn't intend to bring Avery May trouble by coming here. I just wanted to explain and, well, to apologize for Julian's recent behavior." He paused to pet Weasley, who had raised his head in irritation.

"We appreciate your apology," Grandma said. "You don't need to explain your private matters to us."

"No, I want to explain. You *deserve* an explanation. The

problem is, I've been a bit distracted lately with composing. I knew he was getting pretty wrapped up in this new project, but I didn't see that he was getting himself in trouble again."

"Mr. Wayne, am I to understand your boy has been in trouble before?"

"A minor incident at his school is all," he said with a wave of his hand. "He's just passionate. Maybe a little obsessive." He gently removed Weasley's claws from a rip in his jeans. "At any rate, I came here to tell Avery May that Julian was upset when he came back to the house earlier, and that's when he finally told me what was going on."

I squirmed. "What exactly did he tell you?"

"That he tricked you in order to get the reaction he wanted for your ghost film. That's how he gets himself in trouble—he forgets about people's feelings. But he's learning. The very fact that he was upset about *you* being upset was a good sign to me." Curtis Wayne smiled. "Maybe it's just a boy thing, but he's always struggled a little with empathy. You seem to have helped him with that."

And then I called him crazy and told him he should be institutionalized.

I looked at the floor.

"I'm not trying to excuse my son's behavior," Mr. Wayne continued. "Tricking you in that way was unacceptable. Did he tell you he was trying to help you face your fear?"

I nodded.

He glanced at Grandma. "Avery May already knows this, but his mother has been ill for a long time. What I didn't tell Avery is that Julian suffered a trauma when he was younger.

His mother . . . when she was having one of her episodes . . ."
Mr. Wayne swallowed. "Well, she tried to hurt him."

"Dear Lord," breathed Grandma.

"She had some sort of psychotic break in the middle of the night and gave him the scare of his life. He's been in therapy ever since for anxiety, night terrors . . . things like that."

I stared at Mr. Wayne. *Things like that* echoed in my head, sounding small and flimsy. Maybe it was all too big and awful to spell out, especially in front of two kids, but I wanted to know more. I opened my mouth, but Grandma got her words out first.

"I'm truly sorry for your trouble," she said. "May I ask what you meant about Julian trying to help Avery face her fears?"

"He knew from the day he met Avery May that she was frightened of Hilliard House, so he thought by filming there he would help her get over it. At least that was his conscious motivation." He shook his head. "To be honest, I don't understand it completely, but his psychiatrist calls it a reaction formation. His obsession with scary movies and with capturing authentic fear on film . . . well, it's all related to the fact that he's still dealing with a fear he doesn't consciously remember or understand."

Silence fell over the room. Blake leaned back, one eye hidden by the curtain of his too-long hair. Grandma frowned in thought.

Mr. Wayne took a deep breath. "Here I am, going on and on, burdening you with my troubles. I hardly ever talk about it because it's nearly impossible to hold on to one's privacy in my business. I just wanted you to know that things are complicated with Julian. But he's working on it. We're all working on it."

"I do appreciate your candor," Grandma said after a moment. "And I wish nothing but the best for your family." She studied Mr. Wayne before clasping her hands. "Can I get you some iced tea? Or I could put on a pot of coffee, if that's more to your liking."

Mr. Wayne gave Weasley's chin one last scratch before setting him on the floor. "Thank you, but that's not necessary." He stood and brushed the fur from his jeans. "I won't take any more of your time today. I just hope Avery May will come visit us again so that Julian can make his own apologies."

Grandma and I walked him to the breezeway door, and as she called out for him to "come back any time," I gave serious thought to slithering away. Maybe it was best to hide in the attic until she'd cooled down. At that moment, however, Grandma turned around. And she didn't even have to touch me because her tone was sharp enough to pin me down.

"You'd best take a seat in the living room, young lady."

When I came through the doorway, Blake was rising from the rocking chair.

"Sit yourself back down, son," said Grandma.

I sank into the chair Curtis Wayne had occupied, and the warmth of his recent presence settled my nerves a little.

"Avery May, you have a lot of explaining to do. You took my key to Hilliard House that night you were looking through the photo albums, didn't you? Why in heaven's name did you go there when I'd specifically forbidden it?"

I clasped my hands and thought back to my notes on what I'd *intended* to tell Grandma before Mr. Wayne steered us all off course.

"I was going to tell you everything today," I said in my most grown-up voice. "I knew it was wrong to keep secrets."

Her face didn't soften. "Well?"

"Grandma, we have to do something about that house."

She shook her head. "Best to leave it alone. That's what I told you to do in the first place."

"But . . ." I swallowed hard. "It's *haunted*."

She stared at me for a long moment, and I hunkered down for an epic tongue-lashing.

"I know that," she finally said, her voice low and trembling. "Why else would I tell you never to go there?"

CHAPTER 32

"Grandma, you don't believe in ghosts!"

She took a deep breath. "I was brought up to think such notions un-Christian. But the first time I entered that house after Joshua Hilliard's death, I felt him there. I felt his sorrow, his darkness. He didn't want me there, and I've avoided the house ever since. Even that night you were found inside, I couldn't walk through the front door. I was too frightened."

"But it wasn't a scary presence back then. I don't remember much, Grandma, but I know I wasn't frightened."

"I heard her talking to it once," Blake offered. "To *him.* She was happy."

Grandma's eyes narrowed at him. "So you've been keeping secrets, too."

Blake sank back in his chair.

Grandma turned to me. "I don't doubt you were drawn to that presence. He was trying to take you away, just like he tried to take your mother when he was alive. He wanted to replace the little girl he allowed to die."

I shook my head slowly. "I think you're wrong. I think you've been wrong about him all along."

Grandma drew back. "Pardon me?"

"I know you and Grandpa didn't like Joshua Hilliard, but Mom said he was a sweet old gentleman. Too gentle and sad to ever be scary."

Grandma's shoulders softened a smidge.

"I have to go back and talk to Mrs. Shelton," I said. "She knows more than she told us last time."

"I hate for you to bother that poor woman again. Can't you just let this be, Avery May?"

"You want me to give up? What if everyone has been wrong about Joshua Hilliard all this time? Mrs. Shelton said we could come tomorrow morning. But . . . I was hoping you'd take us. It's the only way to put the ghost to rest."

Grandma closed her eyes and sank back into the couch. To see her so slumped and frail made my insides feel hollow.

"Grandma?"

"How on earth are *you* going to put a ghost to rest?"

"I haven't figured that out yet. All I know is you can't sell Hilliard House yet. You can't push that darkness on someone else. That wouldn't be Christianly, would it?"

After a moment she opened her eyes. "No, it wouldn't. But neither can I let a child tackle such a predicament. I simply will not put you in harm's way like that."

"She's not doing it alone," said Blake. "I'm helping."

"For heaven's sake, you're both *children*."

Blake puffed out his chest. "I'm not a kid anymore. And anyway, if you're worried about that, you should come with us."

She sat still for a long time. "It's ridiculous to even consider this. It'd probably be easier just to burn the place down."

I knew better than to answer. I could feel her body soften a little. *Give in,* I thought. *Just this once.*

She gave us a curt nod. "I'll take you to see poor Mrs. Shelton tomorrow morning. That's about all I can promise right now."

Loretta opened the door like before, reeking of cigarette smoke and irritation.

"If it was up to me, you folks wouldn't be here," she said. "But Aunt Aileen is being so bullheaded about it."

I gulped. "Is she angry?"

"No, just feisty." She frowned. "Haven't seen her with this much energy in a long while."

A voice croaked from the bedroom. "Are you going to bring those young'uns in here, or not?"

Loretta herded us in, pulling up a chair for me right next to Mrs. Shelton's bed.

"Get a chair for everyone," said Mrs. Shelton. "And one for yourself, Loretta. We're all going to have squeeze in here somehow, because I want all of you to witness what I have to say today."

She was tiny and shrunken in that bed, but her eyes glinted brightly at Grandma.

"Is that you, Ava? It's been a long time. I suppose it's been more than ten years since I've attended a cemetery cleaning. I can't even get to church anymore, not that I'd see you at a Baptist church anyhow."

I glanced at Grandma, who stared as if her tongue had tied itself.

"Mrs. Shelton," she finally said, "it's awfully generous of you to allow Avery May back in your home. I hope it's not too much trouble."

"Dear lady, it's been a great deal of trouble—in fact, it's been the heaviest of burdens on my mind—but we're about to take care of that, aren't we, Avery May?"

I nodded. I'd been up half the night practicing questions that would cut straight to the truth without crushing old Mrs. Shelton's spirit. Turned out I didn't need them. Aileen Shelton looked ready to take charge of this interview.

"Young man, have you got that little movie camera ready to go?"

"Yes, ma'am."

"Well, then, push Record and I'll start talking."

She cleared her throat and clasped her shaking hands.

"I've been sitting on the truth for over eighty years now. All the people involved have been dead for so long—except me, that is. I figured the truth would go with me to the grave. But when you came here, Avery May, and poked at me with those questions about Meganne and Joshua Hilliard, I felt sick in the heart. And as much as I tried to tell myself the past is past, I knew it'd never gone away. In fact, it's been eating at me all this time."

She paused for a breath, and I didn't dare say a thing. In fact, I willed everyone to keep their traps shut because I knew something big was coming and I didn't want anyone to scare it away.

"I told you my family farmed land owned by Meganne's grandparents," Mrs. Shelton continued. "They had more money than us, and Mama always worried about somehow offending them and losing the land, but they weren't as snobby as they might have been. They bought milk and eggs from us and paid Mama a pretty penny for her quilts. Whenever Mrs. Hilliard visited her folks, Meganne and I were allowed to go off on our own."

Mrs. Shelton paused to cough and clear her throat again. Loretta fussed around, handing her a glass of water and smoothing the edge of her quilt. After taking a sip, Mrs. Shelton waved her off with a frown.

"We had all sorts of adventures in those days. At home, Meganne was watched pretty carefully—I already told you she had a tendency toward puniness, didn't I? Well, when she was with me we rode ponies bareback, milked the goats, gathered eggs, climbed trees, and chased crawdads in the creek. Her fussy mother was none the wiser, and to tell you the truth, I think the fresh air was good for my friend."

A shadow came over her face.

"There came a visit in February when it was too cold and wet to spend time outdoors, and we had to watch over my baby sister, Ruby. Meganne said that if we were to be stuck inside, she wanted to learn how to bake. Her mother always did everything for her—I think she just didn't like for anyone to make a mess in her fancy house—but Meganne wanted to know how to make a cake from scratch for her daddy. Well, I did a fair share of the cooking even at that age. Girls grew up faster then, and Mama made use of me all the time, so I had a good idea what to do. We got the flour, sugar, milk, and butter, and the two of us went out to the henhouse and picked the two prettiest, most perfect eggs we could find. My mama always said *never* to use an egg that was cracked." She pulled a rumpled tissue from the cuff of her gown and pressed it to her lips. "We mixed all that up, little Ruby watching from her high chair, and then I made the mistake of licking the spoon. Would you believe Meganne had never tasted cake batter? So I got out another spoon and let her have a taste. Then Ruby started crying for some. Before I knew it, we were all eating the batter. By the time we'd had our fill, there wasn't enough left to bake the cake, so we just washed the bowl and called it a day.

"Meganne's daddy came to pick her up pretty soon after that. Mrs. Hilliard was staying with her folks for a while because her mother wasn't feeling well, but Meganne had to get back for school. That very night it started raining again, and it didn't let up for days. That was the week everyone talked about when they spoke of the great Carver County flood of 1937.

"On the second day of rain, my baby sister and I started feeling poorly. I mostly just had to keep the bedpan close, but poor Ruby suffered a bad fever and vomiting. And with all the rain, the truck got stuck in a gully, so Mama had to nurse Ruby as best she knew how. She figured out it was the eggs. I told her I picked the uncracked ones, but we know now that the bacteria can be absorbed through the shell."

She cleared her throat again.

"Salmonella," Grandma murmured.

Mrs. Shelton nodded. "Ruby had been underweight and puny to begin with, kind of like Meganne, and—" She paused to swallow. "Well, she didn't make it. Losing my baby sister was quite a blow to Mama. And it wasn't two days later that we learned Meganne had passed away. She'd had fever, aches, and vomiting, just like Ruby. The doctor diagnosed it as typhoid caught from a contaminated well, even though her daddy swore he'd boiled every drop of water she drank. Today a simple test would have revealed the truth, but we didn't have such a thing back then, and everyone was quick to blame the flood for just about anything."

She broke off with coughing again, and after sipping at her water, she wiped her eyes and blew her nose.

"It was a terrible time. All the hens had to be slaughtered, and Mama took me aside and told me never to mention the raw eggs. 'Who's to say it *wasn't* typhoid that took her?' she said. According to her, telling Joshua Hilliard about the eggs wouldn't bring his little girl back, but it *could* take away our livelihood. And hadn't we been punished enough by losing Ruby?

"The truth weighed heavy on me when I heard anyone speak ill of Mr. Hilliard, but I couldn't cross my mother's command. I thought about saying something when Mama died, but by that time Mrs. Hilliard was gone and Mr. Hilliard was a sad shell of a man holed up in that house. And how could I explain keeping silent all those years? I pushed him to the back of my mind, but he's always been waiting there . . . waiting for me to tell the truth." She turned to me. "Avery May, I asked you to bring that photo. May I see it now?"

I fumbled in my pocket and pulled out the silver frame. When she held out her hands, I placed it gently between them.

Mrs. Shelton sighed. "That's a pretty frame."

"Do you need your magnifying glass?" I asked.

"No, honey. I just needed something of hers. I can see her clear as day in my heart."

She stared at that photo for a long moment. Then she spoke to it. "Now, Meganne, I've done it. I've finally told the truth. Can you forgive me?" She sighed heavily. "I'm so sorry. For you. For your daddy." She set the frame down and turned to her niece. "Hand me one of my handkerchiefs, Loretta—these tissues are good for nothing."

We all sat in awkward silence as Mrs. Shelton wiped her face and blew her nose again. Loretta passed the rejected tissue box to Grandma, and that's when I noticed *she'd* been crying, too. Well, I can't see family crying without getting all broken up myself, so when she was done wiping her nose, I gestured for her to pass the box along to me.

"Whew!" breathed Mrs. Shelton. "That's a load off. Haven't felt this light in ages. If it weren't for this heavy quilt, I might just float away."

Loretta peered at her. "Aunt Aileen, do you need a nap?"

"Don't treat me like an infant, Loretta," snapped Mrs. Shelton. "And don't you sit on that information, missy," she said to me. "There's not many people left who remember old Joshua Hilliard, but they should know the truth. He was a good daddy. It was one of many things I envied about Meganne. And that made it all the worse when I saw what happened to him."

"Thank you, Mrs. Shelton. I'll do my best."

"I'll make sure of it," said Grandma.

CHAPTER 33

The drive home was pretty quiet, which gave me time to think through Mrs. Shelton's story. A crazy plan was taking shape in my head, but I waited until we'd started up the hill toward the house before I spoke.

"Grandma, would it be okay if Blake and I visited with Julian? You could just drop us off."

Grandma didn't answer until she'd parked the car in front of Hollyhock Cottage. She looked from Blake to me. "Promise not to go anywhere near Hilliard House without telling me first. I know there's no use trying to keep you away from it now, but I want to be with you when you . . . do whatever it is you're going to do. I need a solemn promise from each of you."

I turned to Blake, and we spoke at the same time. "We promise."

"All right, then. Will you be back for lunch?"

Grandma had never asked that before. It had always been a command, not a question.

"I'm not sure," I said. "Can we call you after we've talked to Julian?"

"That'll be fine."

Blake followed as I stepped up to the front door of the cottage. He grabbed my arm on the top step, raising his eyebrows at the faint sounds of guitar strumming coming from the living room. I shook him off and raised my hand to knock, but the door opened on its own and Julian peered out.

"I saw you from my window."

He was wearing another funky T-shirt, but this one had words on it rather than a cartoon—big white letters that jumped out at you from a black background.

" 'Shoot Films Not People,' " I read aloud. "That's pretty cool. A little creepy, but definitely cool."

Julian leaned against the doorframe. "What do you want, Avery?"

"Um, can we come in?"

"Depends. Are you here to tear my head off? I know Dad ratted us out to your grandmother."

"It's way more complicated than that, Julian. And, yeah, I'm still mad at you, but I'm also sorry, and I need your help." I glanced at Blake. "*We* need your help."

Julian's eyes widened. "You'd better come in, then."

Blake craned his neck toward the living room, but Curtis Wayne didn't even look up from his guitar as we made our way to the stairs. At least his tune sounded a little happier this time.

"Whoa," Blake said at first sight of all the machinery, surge protectors, and snaking power cords in Julian's room. "It's totally what I expected—the lair of an evil genius."

"An evil filmmaking genius." Julian's mouth was a thin line, but his eyes had a little grin to them.

Blake nodded. "I can respect that."

"Okay," I said quickly. "I have something to say to you, Julian."

He raised an eyebrow. "Yeah?"

"I'm sorry I said you were crazy and all." I crossed my arms. Then I uncrossed them because it seemed weird. "I was out of line, and I didn't really mean it. I was super upset that night."

Julian sank into his leather chair. "Okay . . . I'm sorry that I scared you so bad you peed your pants."

"Julian!"

"But it was such a good scene—do you want to see it? I've edited it all together." He looked from me to Blake, and his face crumpled a little. "I really am sorry, Avery."

It wasn't quite the heartfelt apology I'd hoped for, but it would have to do for now, especially since Lily had just walked in. Her eyes widened when she saw me, and I couldn't help noticing that she'd lost a little of her glam. I mean, she was still gorgeous, but she'd ditched the sparkle for a plain white T-shirt and track shorts. Her wild, curly hair was pulled tightly back.

She took one long look at Blake and froze in place.

I sat on the edge of Julian's bed. "I came here to say you were right. There *is* a ghost at Hilliard House—but it's not Margaret Anne."

Julian blinked. "Really?"

"Blake and I are pretty sure we know what's going on. We also know why the ghost is angry." I held out my hand to Lily. "Come sit with me and I'll tell you all about it."

Lily looked from me to Julian and back again. A smile

spread across her face and she crossed the room to curl up next to me. Once she was still, I explained our Internet research on ghosts. Then I shared Aileen Shelton's story of what really happened to Margaret Anne.

"Wow," Julian said. "So her death had nothing to do with the flood or Mr. Hilliard?"

I shook my head. "If you hadn't pushed me into making a ghost movie, and if you and Lily hadn't tricked me, we never would have learned how Joshua Hilliard had been wronged all these years. And now maybe I have a chance to fix it so that people can live in that house again."

Lily looked up at me. "How?"

"That presence in the house needs to hear the truth from Aileen Shelton."

"But she can't leave her bed, Avery," Blake said.

"She doesn't have to."

He frowned. "I don't get it."

"I have an idea, but it's going to take some time to work it out. I need your trust on this, Blake. Are you with me?"

After a moment he nodded.

"I'll need help from all of you." I turned to Julian. "Especially you."

Julian straightened in his chair. "Maybe Lily could scrounge up something for us to eat while we work. There's some peanut butter and crackers in the pantry."

Lily looked from him to me. "Avery, you want to come with me?"

"I can't right now. But I bet Blake would be glad to help after he calls Grandma."

Blake swept the hair out of his eyes and glared at me. But when he caught Lily watching him, his frown softened. "No problem."

"Thanks. I have to check with Julian on some stuff, but I promise I'll explain everything when you guys get back with the food. We just *have* to get this ready to go by tomorrow."

"Then we'd better get cracking," Julian said.

CHAPTER 34

On an ordinary Sunday, church seemed to last forever, but I figured it'd feel like two forevers that morning. Brother Wilson didn't help matters with his long-winded announcements. Eventually he reached for the prayer box, which was the last step before the sermon. Every week members of the congregation stuffed that box with prayer requests for sick loved ones, upcoming surgeries, traveling mercies, and other such things. Grandma never contributed—at least not when Blake and I came to church with her. Whether that had to do with pride or privacy, I wasn't sure. I figured if she was going to ask for prayers, it would be for her daughter's soul, but if she did that, it would be like admitting her own failure. So she kept those thoughts to herself.

That morning, however, her name came up first.

"Mrs. Hilliard asks that everyone please pray for Joshua Hilliard, her husband's cousin who's been dead for thirty years."

I could feel every head in church turning to stare at Grandma. She took a handkerchief out of her pocketbook and dabbed at her eyes.

Brother Wilson read the piece of paper in silence. Then he

glanced at Grandma, who nodded firmly. He raised his chin. "Folks, this is a long one, and it's probably best I read it word for word, just as Mrs. Hilliard wrote it."

He cleared his throat.

"'For many years, I was convinced that Mr. Hilliard was a man with a dark soul. A man who lost his child through neglect and thereafter drove his wife to an early grave. I didn't even know him until long after his daughter and wife died, but I confess to having judged him and even indulged in gossip about him, both when he was alive and after he passed. Yesterday I learned the truth about Joshua Hilliard. He had nothing to do with his daughter's death. He was, in fact, a loving father. But because certain people held silent, he was judged harshly and incorrectly by the entire community. I only learned this because of research conducted by my grandchildren.'"

Grandma placed a hand on each of our shoulders, and I felt several pairs of eyes settling on me.

Brother Wilson folded the paper and looked upon the congregation. "Mrs. Hilliard concludes her request by asking us to pray not only for Joshua Hilliard, but also for her and for all those who judge without having all the facts."

After that I barely heard the other prayer requests, my head and heart were so full of Grandma's words. Just when I was pretty sure I had her all figured out, she pulled a stunt like this—and even though she didn't speak the words, they rang out with her brand of truth. You'd think a grandma's job was to be steady and predictable, but she'd been surprising me all summer. I was tempted to give her a powerful squeeze in front of the entire congregation, but I knew such a public display would only embarrass the heck out of her.

"That was hard-core," Blake said as we climbed into the car afterward.

"The only way it could have been better," I said, "is if Grandma had actually stood up and spoken herself. Brother Wilson would have freaked!"

Grandma glanced at me in the rearview mirror. "You know I would never do that, Avery May."

I swallowed. "Sorry, ma'am."

Grandma put her key in the ignition but paused before starting the car. "Your mother broke from the church because she felt oppressed by our traditions, but I want you two to know that all the women of Sycamore Road Church of Christ are strong and opinionated. We follow scripture by choice. Am I understood?"

"Yes, ma'am," Blake and I said together.

Grandma offered no further comment on the matter and held quiet on the drive home. Once we'd changed out of our church clothes, she handed me the cordless phone to call Julian. He and Lily were at the door in less than ten minutes.

Grandma shook her head at the sight of Lily in her bejeweled cap and flip-flops. "Isn't she a bit young for . . . what we're doing today?"

"But I've already been in the house lots of times," Lily said.

Julian laid a hand on her shoulder. "Mrs. Hilliard's right, Lil. You can walk with us, but I want you to wait outside once we get to the house."

"Jules!"

I shot a desperate look at Blake.

"I'll wait outside with you, Lily," he said quickly.

A slow smile spread across her face. "Okay, then."

Grandma drove to the house. The rest of us walked, and I was happy to let Blake take the lead. Nobody spoke at first. I guess we were all trying to imagine exactly what we'd find inside Hilliard House. My heart thumped with the knowledge that we *finally* were doing the right thing, but at the same time dread pitted in my belly. We were about to walk into the house of a suffering spirit. An angry spirit.

"You know," I said to Julian, "once we're in the house, it's probably best not to stand too long under a light fixture or in a doorway. Best to just march straight to the parlor, and that way there won't be time for any funny business."

"I have my camera in this backpack," he said. "Maybe I could get a real ghost on film."

I stopped in my tracks. "Julian, you can't."

"Why not?"

"It's not why we're doing this. You'd be taking advantage."

"It could be *historic*."

I glared at him. "Will you ever *learn*?"

Ahead of us, Blake turned around. "What's the holdup, Avery?"

"You and Lily go ahead," I said. "We'll catch up in a second. I just need to work through a few details with Julian."

I tried to send a powerful psychic message to Blake. *It's okay. Just go on.* Not sure he got it, though, because his an-

noyed expression didn't soften. But after a moment he nodded at Lily and they continued on.

I turned back to Julian.

He raised his hands in surrender. "Okay, you're right. I'd
probably make the ghost mad if I tried to get it on film. I got
a little carried away, I guess. . . ."

"Seems like you get carried away a lot."

He looked away without answering.

"Julian, what did your mom do that scared you so bad?"

He turned back to me, eyes wide. After a moment he
shook his head. "Dad has a big mouth."

I held his gaze, waiting.

He sighed. "I'll tell you while we walk, but let's hang back
a little. Lily doesn't know much about my mother, and I'd
rather keep it that way for now."

I'd sprung that question on him out of the blue, and in
a different situation I might have given him a moment to
pull himself together. But we didn't have far to go before we
reached Hilliard House, so I gently bumped his arm as we
walked. "Well?"

"I don't remember much," he said, "but I guess when I
was about five my mother came to my room in the middle of
the night, and she, um . . ."

"She what?"

"She tried to smother me."

My scalp prickled. "Seriously?"

"I told you she was sick. Still *is* sick. Anyway, Dad had
been out of town for a while, but he was there that night,
sleeping on the couch. He must have heard the struggle. He

says he took me to the bathroom and locked the door. Then he called the police."

"But why would she do that?"

"She said she was following God's command."

"*What?*"

"She said God spoke to her directly, and in her mind he'd given me the fast pass to Heaven."

I shook my head. "I'd never be able to sleep again after that sort of thing."

"Yeah, my therapist says I fixate on fear and scary movies as a coping mechanism."

"Wait, are you saying you scare *other* people in order to make yourself feel better?"

"Strange, huh? I guess it's a control thing—if I'm the one who finds or creates the scary thing, it can't hurt me." He frowned. "But I never go into it thinking 'I want to scare someone.'"

"Did you scare somebody at school? Did you *bully* someone?"

"What? *No.*"

"But you got in trouble, didn't you? Don't give me that look—your dad was trying to explain to Grandma why you tricked me at Hilliard House. That's the only reason I know you got in trouble."

"It's not what you think, but it's kind of hard to explain." He sighed. "When you're at school, do you ever feel like you're in a horror film?"

"Huh . . . I never actually thought of it that way."

"After I took that summer class on filmmaking, I started filming at school because there was so much drama there.

You know, kids arguing at their lockers. Teachers bellowing down the hall. One day I saw this boy getting bullied in the lunchroom. I knew him a little—he was one of those kids who's small for his age and makes up for it with a smart mouth. Some bigger guys surrounded him, and one of them stood so the teachers couldn't really see. They were thumping his head and pushing his face into his mashed potatoes. I watched the whole thing through the camera on my tablet."

I shook my head. "You were filming it?"

"When I got home and watched the footage that night, it was . . . powerful. When that boy sat there with mashed potatoes on his face, crying, it was pure, raw emotion. I made some edits, gave it a title, and posted it to the school's Facebook page."

"For real?"

He nodded. "It was *important*. I was shining a light on a problem in our school, right? I wanted that kid to know that he shouldn't let stupid bullies have that kind of power over him. But the kid's parents didn't see it that way and raised a big stink. The principal went ballistic. And I got suspended."

It took a minute for all that to soak in.

"Are you back to thinking I'm crazy?" he asked.

I really just wanted to push *his* face in a plate of mashed potatoes to smash some sense into him. Instead I made myself think through my words. "You talk about the risks an artist has to take, but will you do me a favor? Next time you're about to take a risk for a film, ask yourself if it would hurt someone else."

He grimaced. "You sound like my therapist."

"I just don't want you to get in trouble anymore. I mean, we might have more movies to make together."

He ducked his head, so I couldn't be sure how he felt about that suggestion.

"Come on." I tried to make my tone light. "We should catch up with Blake and Lily."

CHAPTER 35

Hilliard House stood tall and gloomy under gray clouds, its narrow door like a puckered mouth holding back secrets. Grandma's little blue car looked out of place in the driveway, as if it had traveled through a wormhole to the past. Our plan had sounded pretty crazy in theory, and now that it was actually happening, my courage was ready to sneak out through a back alley.

Grandma stepped out of the car and slammed the door. "I forgot the key."

I glanced at Julian. "I think we left the door unlocked last time. We, um, got a little spooked."

"I suppose I'd better brace myself for damage, among other things." She wiped her damp face with a handkerchief.

We fell into line on the brick path, Blake leading the way. At the foot of the steps he came to a halt and turned. "Who's going to open the door?"

I glanced at Julian.

He nodded encouragingly.

I straightened my spine. "I should do it."

The knob was a little cold to the touch, but the longer I held it, the warmer it got. I gently leaned against the door, trying to think friendly thoughts. *We just want to help,* I said in my head over and over. Finally the knob turned, and the door opened. The light fixture still lay sprawled on the floor, and that rush of sadness came at me again, making me shiver.

Julian was right behind me. "Man, that really hits you in the gut."

I stepped around the fallen fixture and waved at Grandma to come in. As she crossed over the threshold, the temperature dropped. I looked beyond her to where Blake and Lily stood at the edge of the porch. Without even looking up at him, Lily slipped her hand into Blake's.

"Are you okay?" Blake called out.

I gave the thumbs-up. Then I went straight to the staircase and gathered up the doll, placing the head carefully on its soft midsection. With my free hand I reached for Grandma. "You all right?"

She nodded, and I swear I heard her teeth chatter. I squeezed her hand tightly and looked around me. When we'd run out of the house last time, the double doors on either side of us had been shut. Or at least I thought they had. Now they were open.

"We'll do this in the parlor," I said. "That's where they found me all those years ago, wasn't it, Grandma?"

"They said you were asleep on the floor, right in front of the fireplace."

The words were barely out of her mouth before I heard a familiar creaking. The air around us stilled, and I watched Julian's jaw drop as if it were happening in slow motion. My ears ached from a sudden pressure.

I squeezed Grandma's hand and braced myself.

Every door in the house slammed shut.

Grandma gasped and pulled me to her. I could feel her trembling, hear the thumping of her heart. Julian sidled over to us, his eyes wide. Just outside the front door Blake shouted and rattled the knob.

"Stop it, Blake!" I shouted.

There was a moment of quiet. All I could hear was our breathing.

Then the doors on either side of us began to shake, slowly at first, then faster, louder, as if dark, wild creatures were desperate to get at us.

"You have to leave, Julian!" I shouted. "You too, Grandma."

She shook her head, squeezing me tighter. "You're coming with me."

I gently pried her arms off me and took her hand, giving her a steady look. "If the doors don't stop shaking, I won't go in the parlor. I promise I'll follow you." I turned to Julian. "Please take her outside."

Julian stared. Then he walked toward the front door. Straightening his shoulders, he reached for the knob, turning it quickly. The door opened without a problem.

"Go," I said to Grandma. "If everything calms down, and I'm pretty sure it will, I'll go into the parlor alone."

She squeezed my hand so hard I thought my bones might crack.

The doors shook even harder.

"I can't let you walk into danger!" she shouted. "Just come with us. We'll figure out a different plan."

I leaned in, rising on my toes to speak into her ear.

"Grandma, I'm the only one who can talk to Mr. Hilliard. I've done it before, and he didn't touch a hair on my head. I must have felt pretty safe if I fell asleep in this house."

"Let me come in there with you, then."

I shook my head. "Trust me, Grandma. You'll be able to see me through the window."

Her eyes said lots of things to me in the next few seconds. They spoke of her fear, but also of her love. She pulled me close for an instant. Then she let go and turned away, and I could hear her praying as she followed Julian out the front door.

CHAPTER 36

As soon as the front door slammed shut, the horrible rattling eased.

"It's just me now," I said softly.

The doors on either side of me stilled entirely, and a silence fell over the house. That strange despair still twisted in my gut like nausea, but it no longer lapped over me in waves. I took a breath and stepped to the parlor doors, touching my fingers to the right-hand doorknob.

"Let me in? *Please.*"

The knob warmed and turned easily for me. I took another deep breath, bracing myself. Then I pushed the door open and walked through.

I paused at the edge of the room. After all the crazy rattling, I half expected the room to be a wreck, but nothing looked out of place. The room *felt* different, though, as if it was a living thing that had been crouching in wait, its muscles tensed for decades.

A knock at the window made me jump. I slowly stepped toward it, easing the yellowed curtains open. Grandma and Julian stood just outside, with Blake peering over their shoulders.

I nodded. *I'm okay.*

Grandma clasped her hands to her mouth.

I turned to face the fireplace. The dusty old rug lay in front of it, and I tried to remember lying there, falling asleep. The memory hovered at the edge of my mind, but at this point I doubted I'd ever catch it.

I shrugged out of my knapsack and eased it to the floor by the fireplace. Then I took the doll and placed her body on the left side of the mantel, gently setting the head on top. Once the doll was arranged, I pulled the photograph of Margaret Anne and Aileen out of the knapsack and set it on the right side of the mantel.

Within seconds the room turned cooler.

I pulled one last item from the knapsack—Julian's tablet. We'd rehearsed a quick opening of the file, but my hands were shaking as I expanded it to full screen. When it was ready to go, I set it on the mantel between the doll and the photograph, just below the framed picture of the first Hilliard House.

"I want to show you something," I said.

Silence was my only answer.

"When we first came here, we had the story all wrong. I think we've got it right this time."

I tapped Play on the tablet and stepped back as the light from the screen brightened the room.

The film opened with Blake's wide shot of the cemetery, just as I'd planned several nights ago in the attic. Julian and I had sifted through all our clips to find the best footage, and he'd edited them so they'd flow more smoothly. He'd also added an antique filter that made the whole thing look like an old film.

The camera moved in on me standing near the cemetery sign, and it was odd to hear this black-and-white version of myself talk about the Hilliard family and how they'd settled the area. When the camera focused on Elizabeth and Margaret Anne's gravestone, I felt a shift in the air. It wasn't a change in temperature—more like a static charge. My hair seemed to lift a little, and my heart pounded faster.

The scene moved to Hilliard House, with Blake's footage of me talking about Joshua Hilliard's life. Blake and I had coaxed Grandma into letting us use the photographs from Grandpa's albums, so while I spoke of Joshua's time at war and his marriage to Elizabeth Anne, the scanned images smoothly transitioned in and out.

During a close-up of Margaret Anne and her dandelion hair, I glanced sidelong at the old framed photograph above the mantel and saw a flicker in the glass. My heartbeat quickened, but I couldn't bring myself to turn around. When I looked at the photograph straight on, nothing was there.

Now Mrs. Shelton appeared and spoke of Margaret Anne's visits to the farm. The air around me shifted again, this time as if a storm was gathering in the parlor. A chill concentrated right behind me, and my ears popped.

He was there.

Every hair on my body lifted as I fought the urge to back out of the room.

I focused on the video again. When Mrs. Shelton spoke of eggs, batter, and death, the pressure in my ears almost became unbearable, and that familiar wave of sorrow washed over me until I thought I might drown in it. Just as I was about to curl up on the floor and sob, it stopped. The final scene was rolling, and there I stood under a tree speaking directly to Joshua Hilliard. It was the last thing we'd filmed before Julian and I started editing.

"I never really knew you, Mr. Hilliard," said the film version of me. "You died before I was born, but you were a friend to my mom when she was a lonely girl growing up on the farm. I think you were a friend to me when I was little, though I still can't remember. I'm sorry you never knew what really made your daughter sick. I'm sorry that others blamed you for her death, when it was something out of your control. I'm sorry you spent your life afraid they might be right. And I'm sorry that members of my own family thought you were a bad person. We know the truth now. I hope that lots of people will see this and understand. But most of all, I hope you can rest in peace."

I let out the breath I'd been holding, expecting the screen to fade to black. A title rolled instead—Julian must have added it after I'd left the cottage.

GHOSTLIGHT
BY
AVERY MAY HILLIARD

Behind the words was an image of a lighted window. The light flickered, and then the screen went blank. It was a small thing, but so perfect that my eyes started to prickle.

For a moment all was still. I held my breath, waiting for . . . I didn't know what.

Then I felt a slight pressure on my right shoulder, as if a hand lightly rested there. I couldn't turn my head—my body had seized up—but I glanced at the framed photograph and saw the shadowy outline reflected in the glass. My heart pounded so hard that even my lips were trembling, but I did my best to smile.

The shadow vanished.

"Good-bye," I whispered.

CHAPTER 37

When we were certain the calm was real and lasting, we took some time setting things right in the house. Blake and I collected broken bits of light fixture and dragged them outside, while Julian and Lily grabbed old towels from the car to clean the upstairs bathroom. Grandma took a broom to the worst of the dust and mouse droppings.

"Once the cleaners are gone tomorrow," she said, "we need to find the mouse holes and plug them up. You know I don't hold with poison or traps."

We went from room to room, opening curtains and shades, sweeping up mouse droppings and dead flies, all the while collecting small bits that Grandma wanted to save. When she and I came to the room with the sad old bed frame, I lifted the corner of the quilt to show her. "This was made by Aileen Shelton's mother. See the initials?" I pointed to the embroidered s.f. "I don't know her first name, but the last name was Forney. It's got to be hers, right?"

"Seems likely," Grandma said.

I ran my finger along the tiny, even stitches of the flowery patches. "May I have it? And take it back to Dallas?"

Grandma reached out to touch the torn binding. "You'll

have to sew up the damaged areas first. I'll show you how, and you can do your work in the sewing room. Then you'll have to take care with washing it and hanging it out to dry." She put her hand on my shoulder. "It'll be a lot of work. Are you prepared for that?"

I nodded. "I really want it."

"All right, then."

When we took the quilt downstairs, we found Lily standing alone in the parlor. She stared up at the doll.

"You were right, Lily," I said. "Mrs. Shelton told me she *was* Margaret Anne's doll."

Lily nodded without looking at me. "Does she have a name?"

"Bettina. She came all the way from Germany as a present from Margaret Anne's daddy."

Lily turned to Grandma. "I broke it that night we scared Avery."

Grandma moved to the mantel and reached toward the doll.

"The head's just sitting on top," I said quickly.

Grandma gently brought the head down and studied it. "There's a crack in the back of the hair, but we could fill that. And it's easy enough to anchor the head back on."

"It also needs its stuffing replaced," Lily said. "A mouse got to it."

Grandma placed the head in Lily's hands. "Come over to the house and I'll show you how to sew up the body and wash her clothes. You won't be able to play with her—she's too delicate for that—but you could set her on a shelf and admire her. She's very old and precious."

Lily looked into the doll's eyes. "I want to fix her, but . . . she belongs here. Do you think the new owner would take her?"

Grandma smiled. "Maybe we could make a shadow box for her. Then we could offer it as a housewarming present. Now that I think of it, I have plastic and paper bags in the trunk of the car. Avery, why don't you and Lily get those doll pieces wrapped up for the drive home?"

On the way out we passed Blake sweeping the front hallway. He paused to wink at Lily, reaching out to tweak one of her curls. She giggled.

As soon as we were on the brick path leading down to the car, Lily looked up at me, her eyes shy. "Your brother is so cute."

I groaned. "He's a little old for you, don't you think?"

"Well, he is *now*. But when I'm twenty-one, he'll be . . . twenty-seven, I think?"

"Yeah, that sounds about right."

She sighed. "We could get married then."

"You really do like to plan ahead, don't you?" I opened the driver's side door of Grandma's car to pop the trunk. "Well, I can't imagine anyone wanting to marry Blake. For one thing, his feet are really smelly."

"But he's tall, and strong, and smart . . ."

"Um, I'm not so sure about that last one."

"Well, *you're* smart, and he's your brother, right? Your mom must be smart 'cause she's a lawyer. I bet your dad is pretty smart, too." She looked back at the house. "Does Blake look like him?"

I shut the car door a little too hard. Then I turned to follow her gaze to where Blake stood in the doorway, sweeping dirt and bits of broken glass into a dustpan.

Mom and I had dark hair, but Blake's was kind of medium blond. Mom's eyes were brown, but Blake's and mine were blue. Blake was already way taller than Mom, who was petite like me. Why had I never asked myself where his blond hair, blue eyes, and long legs came from?

I turned back to Lily. "I never thought about it before, but yeah. I'm pretty sure Blake *does* look like our dad."

She smiled. "That's cool."

I glanced at Blake again. He was staring at the full dustpan like he really just wanted to dump it on the grass. But then he sighed and walked it into the house, probably to find the big garbage can Grandma had set up in the kitchen.

"Actually, Lily, it *is* cool." I pulled her close and kissed the top of her head. "It really is."

By the time we'd sorted the trash from the keepsakes and carried it all out to Grandma's car, the sky was rumbling with thunder and every belly groaned from hunger.

"Looks like it might finally rain, so let's head on back," Grandma said. "I have enough chicken and squash casserole in the Crock-Pot to feed us all twice over." She turned to Julian. "As soon as we get to the house, I'll call your daddy and invite him, too. That man is too skinny for my liking."

Julian nodded.

"Lily can ride back with me, but the rest of you have to

walk. The car is too full of that thing's innards." Grandma raised her head to consider the house. "It's mighty handsome, though, isn't it? Two days ago I couldn't wait to be rid of it, but now I'm a little sad to say good-bye."

"Why can't you just keep it, Mrs. Hilliard?" Lily asked.

"Sweetie, I can barely keep up with my own business, that's why. I don't have the energy to give this house the attention it needs." She wiped her hands on her slacks. "I believe the buyers have grand plans."

"Is a big family buying it?" I asked.

She shook her head. "A young married couple. The wife grew up in these parts, and they want to turn it into a bed-and-breakfast. Good luck to them, I say. It's quite an under-taking." She patted Lily on the head. "Come on, sweetie. Let's go eat."

Blake and Julian were quiet on the walk back to Grandma's house, and the silence made me squirmy. I guess it wasn't easy to make small talk after you'd laid a ghost to rest *and* busted your behind to clean his house afterward.

My thoughts stayed with Hilliard House as we walked. We'd left it a little tidier than we found it, but I longed to see how the house might shine if the right people put hard work and love into it. I imagined gleaming floors, polished wood-work, and fresh wallpaper. Floral curtains and beds made up with bright quilts and frilly bed skirts. Old-fashioned framed prints and photographs hanging on the walls. I saw the dining room filled with guests who'd worked up an appetite exploring the hills and hollows of Carver County. People hungry for history and interesting tales.

"Oh," I breathed.

Blake nudged my shoulder. "What?"

It took a moment to untangle my thoughts. "Do you remember when I told Mom that Julian and I were making a film on the history of this area? She said it would be nice for Grandma's website, to help draw interest to the rental cottage."

"Yeah, but Grandma won't get a website."

"She should," Julian said. "I bet you the new owners of Hilliard House will make one."

"Exactly," I said.

Julian shook his head. "Your grandma might lose business because of that."

"That's what I've been thinking about. What if they included Grandma's cottage on their website?"

"Why would they?" Blake asked.

"Because we'll make it worth their while," I said. "I have an idea for a short film—maybe several films—each of them about some bit of history around here. But the films would be about people and their stories. Local lore and all that. It's what visitors come here for. We could start with Hilliard House and Joshua Hilliard. We have plenty of footage on that already. We could sort of hint at the ghost, you know? And there might be more old-timey Carver County stories we could work with, too."

Julian's eyes brightened. "Interesting."

"I bet Grandma would let us use her photos again, and we could do research at the library. By the time Hilliard House was ready to open, we'd have a bunch of short films for their website. And, Julian, if you edit them like you did this film for Joshua Hilliard, they'd be begging for them. They might even pay us."

"Sounds like a lot of work," Blake muttered. "We can't do it all this summer."

"And I might not be back next summer," Julian said.

I came to halt. "Come on, guys, you know it's a great idea! Can we at least work on the Hilliard House video and see how that turns out? It would be a great way to do what Mrs. Shelton wanted. We'd be letting people know that Joshua Hilliard was a good man."

Blake shook his hair into his eyes and walked on, but Julian turned to look back at the house.

"It could work," he said.

We stared at the house in silence for a moment.

"By the way," I said, "nice touch with the title credit on the movie. When did you slip that in?"

"Thought you'd like that. I put it together this morning and added it as a surprise." He gave me a sidelong look. "And as an apology."

CHAPTER 38

It seemed a little strange that a girl could be guiding a ghost to the beyond one day and crouching in the garden to pick green beans the next, but that's exactly how it went down. Easing back into the mindless and ordinary actually proved to be a comfort, and I think Blake felt it, too. He didn't grouch at me once, even though he'd lost his blackmail advantage in the garden, *and* Grandma had given us both dish duty for the rest of the summer. The morning was downright cheerful, especially now that the air felt cool and light after the rain. I hardly minded the mud at all.

"Hey, I've been thinking," Blake said.

"Yeah?"

"We still have half the summer left. We should start some sort of project."

I flicked a green bean at him. "We already *have* a project. The Legends of Carver County, remember?"

He snorted. "That's not my project. That's for you and the evil genius."

"Then *what*? I can't stand football, and I'm not going to help you with your summer-reading questions."

"That's not what I meant."

I sat back and stared at him. "You're not saying we should start up with Kingdom again, are you?"

He shook his head. "We're both so *over* that—you said it yourself. Plus, I really don't want to go back to you trying to boss me around all the time."

"I never bossed you!"

He laughed. "Are you kidding me? You still don't get it, do you? *You* made all the rules with Kingdom. *You* decided who the characters were. *You* scripted it all out yourself. I was just there because *you* couldn't play all the characters at the same time."

"You created some of the characters," I said after a moment.

"Yeah, but you always had to change something about them."

"I don't remember that."

"And when I tried to tell you I was done, you *punished* me," he said.

"Oh, come on," I muttered. "I'm not falling for your victim act. You were rude to me *and* you blackmailed me. Twice in one week!"

"Okay, so neither of us is perfect. I own my faults, but you've got to own yours, too."

"*Own my faults?* You sound like a talk show."

"You know what I mean."

I sighed. "Yeah."

Blake's eyes brightened. "Speaking of shows, you know what would be cool? If we did something like *Ghosthunter Teens*. A show about catching ghosts in action, only with us doing the investigating instead of those old bald guys. I bet there's all sorts of hauntings around here." He frowned. "It'd be better if I could drive, though."

"I don't know, Blake. I've probably had enough ghost encounters to last me for a long while."

"What about a spoof? It would be totally funny. And we wouldn't actually have to find any ghosts. Maybe our team could specialize in kid ghosts, and then . . ."

I just kept picking beans while he rattled on about his wacky ghost show. It was nice to have him talking again. It was nice to have him acting like Blake again.

Or maybe he'd been the same Blake all along and it was me who'd gotten weird.

How did I go back to being Avery again? And what did that even mean?

I could imagine Mom's answer to that question. She'd say being Avery didn't mean bossing or punishing my brother just because he didn't see things the same way I did. It couldn't mean lying and stealing from Grandma, either. And it shouldn't ever mean being so desperate for attention that I'd blindly follow someone else straight into trouble.

To me, being Avery meant loving stories. On the page, on the screen, and in my head before I went to sleep at night. Before this summer, all I'd wanted was to escape into tales of people from past times and unusual places. But what about unusual people who lived in ordinary places? In the here and now?

What about a dreamy girl with no father but more family than she knew what to do with?

A girl who was betrayed but learned to forgive . . .

A girl who helped a ghost move on . . .

What would happen next in her story?

ACKNOWLEDGMENTS

Heartfelt gratitude goes to:

—Michelle Frey and the editorial team at Knopf, for helping me poke and prod *Ghostlight* into tip-top shape.

—Jennifer Laughran, for being a tireless advocate, story genius, and dear friend.

—Katrina Damkoehler, for the perfectly creepy cover design.

—Brandi Barnett, Kelly Bristow, Martha Bryant, Dee Dee Chumley, Mari Farthing, Kim Harrington, Shel Harrington, Lisa Marotta, Helen Newton, and Natalie Parker, for their friendship and story feedback.

—Bethany Hegedus, Sara Zarr, and all the participants in the 2013 Writing Barn workshop on "Emotional Pacing," for helping me hone those critical first three chapters.

—Vicki Hill and Connie Peacher, for clarifying pertinent details regarding the Church of Christ.

—Dr. Lisa Marotta and Dr. Terry Peacher (hey, Dad!), for consulting on Julian Wayne's diagnosis.

—Marcia and J. Trekell, my mom and stepfather, for helping me remember the night sounds of Stewart County, Tennessee (the inspiration for Carver County).

—Ruby Peacher, my grandmother, for inspiring me with stories and photographs of the 1937 floods.

—Ernest, Heather, Jason, Dionne, York, Shelby, and Samantha—my siblings and nieces—for providing me with a lifetime of data on sibling dynamics. Big hugs to each of you!

—All my dear friends and family members who offered love and support. I'm so lucky to have you.

—My husband, Steve, for going above and beyond with this manuscript, giving feedback on multiple drafts—chapter-by-chapter, word-by-word. Thank you for supporting me from the moment I hatched this crazy plan to be a writer, and for growing more enthusiastic about my career with each new book. None of this could have happened without you, and I thank you for sharing this journey with me. I love you. Forever.

ABOUT THE AUTHOR

Sonia Gensler is the author of two young adult novels: *The Dark Between,* which *School Library Journal* called "vivid and intriguing," and *The Revenant,* winner of the Oklahoma Book Award and a Parents' Choice Silver Award.

Sonia grew up in a small Tennessee town and spent her early adulthood collecting impractical degrees from various midwestern universities. A former high school English teacher, she now writes full-time in Oklahoma. You can find out more at soniagensler.com.